this

is not

a   n   o   v   e   l

david markson

THIS IS
NOT A
NOVEL

COUNTERPOINT

WASHINGTON, D.C.

Library of Congress Cataloging-in-Publication Data
Markson, David
This is not a novel / David Markson.—1st Counterpoint pbk.ed.
p.   cm.
ISBN 1-58243-133-7 (alk. paper)
I. Title.
PS3563.A67 T48 2001
818'.5407—dc21   00-064444

FIRST PRINTING

COUNTERPOINT
P.O. Box 65793
Washington, D.C. 20035–5793

Counterpoint is a member of the Perseus Books Group.

10 9 8 7 6 5 4 3 2 1

For Toby and Duncan Freeman

and Sydney Markson

I am now trying an Experiment very
frequent among Modern Authors;
which is, to *write upon Nothing.*

—Swift

this is not

Writer is pretty much tempted to quit writing.

Writer is weary unto death of making up stories.

Lord Byron died of either rheumatic fever, or typhus, or
uremia, or malaria.
Or was inadvertently murdered by his doctors, who had
bled him incessantly.

Stephen Crane died of tuberculosis in 1900. Granted an
ordinary modern life span, he would have lived well into
World War II.

This morning I walked to the place where the street-
cleaners dump the rubbish. My God, it was beautiful.
Says a van Gogh letter.

Writer is equally tired of inventing characters.

Bertolt Brecht died of a stroke. Terrified of being buried
alive, he had pleaded that a stiletto be driven through his
heart once he was declared legally dead. An attending
physician did so.

a   n   o   v   e   l

1

Mr. Coleridge, do not cry. If opium really does you any good, and you must have it, why do you not go and get it?
Asked Wilkie Collins' mother.

William Blake lived and dressed in inconceivable filth, and virtually never bathed.
Mr. Blake's skin don't dirt, his wife Catherine contributed.

When I was their age I could draw like Raphael. But it took me a lifetime to learn to draw like they do.
Said Picasso at an exhibition of children's art.

A novel with no intimation of story whatsoever, Writer would like to contrive.

And with no characters. None.

The Globe Theatre burned to the ground on June 29, 1613. Did any new play of Shakespeare's, not yet in quarto publication, perhaps burn with it?

Albert Camus, on the one occasion when he was introduced to William Faulkner:
The man did not say three words to me.

Nietzsche died after a sequence of strokes. But his final illness, and his madness, were almost surely the result of syphilis.

W. H. Auden was once arrested for urinating in a public park in Barcelona.

Frans Hals was once arrested for beating his wife.

Plotless. Characterless.

Yet seducing the reader into turning pages nonetheless.

No one was injured in the Globe Theatre calamity. One man's breeches were set on fire, but it is on record that the flames were quenched with a tankard of ale.

When Dickens shocked Victorian London by separating from his wife, it was Thackeray who let slip that it was over an actress. Dickens did not speak to him for years.

Tell it not in Gath, publish it not in the streets of Askelon.

George Santayana, reading *Moby Dick:*
In spite of much skipping, I have got stuck in the middle.

Thales of Miletus died at his seat while watching an athletic contest.

But I knew that Monsieur Beyle quite well, and you will never convince me that a trifler like him could have written masterpieces.
Said Sainte-Beuve.

Actionless, Writer wants it.

Which is to say, with no *sequence of events*.

Which is to say, with no indicated *passage of time*.

Then again, getting somewhere in spite of this.

The old wives' tale, repeated by Socrates, that Thales
was also frequently so preoccupied with gazing up at the
stars that he once tumbled into a well.
And was even laughed at by washerwomen.

Jack Donne, the young John Donne was commonly
called.

Oedipus gouges out his eyes, Jocasta hangs herself, both
guiltless; the play has come to a harmonious conclusion.
Wrote Schiller.

Verdi died of a stroke.

Puccini died of throat cancer.

Indeed, with a beginning, a middle, and an end.

Even with a note of sadness at the end.

What porridge had John Keats?
Asked Browning.

What is the use of being kind to a poor man?
Asked Cicero.

Bertrand Russell was so inept, physically, that he could never learn to make a pot of tea.
Immanuel Kant could not manage to sharpen a quill pen with a penknife.
John Stuart Mill could barely tie a simple knot.

The sixth-century legend that St. Luke was a painter.
And did a portrait of the Virgin Mary.

Tartini's violin.
Which shattered in its case at his death.

Insistently, Brahms wore his pants too short.
Sometimes actually taking a scissors to the bottoms.

A novel with no *setting*.

With no so-called furniture.

Ergo meaning finally without *descriptions*.

André Gide died of a disease of the lungs.
Rereading the *Aeneid* on his deathbed.

It was while they were making copies of the Masaccio frescoes in the Santa Maria del Carmine as young apprentices that Michelangelo criticized the draftsmanship of Pietro Torrigiano:

Bone and cartilage went down like biscuit, Torrigiano would later tell Benvenuto Cellini.

Re Michelangelo's nose.

The greatest genius of our century, Goethe called Byron.

The greatest genius of our century, Byron called Goethe.

Ivan Turgenev, at nineteen, during a shipboard fire: Save me! I am my mother's only son!

Catullus, who loved a woman he called Lesbia, but whose real name may have been Clodia.

Propertius, who loved a woman he called Cynthia, but whose real name may have been Hostia.

Both, two full thousand years ago.

Gustav Mahler died of endocarditis.

Louis-Ferdinand Céline died of a brain aneurysm.

A novel with no overriding central *motivations*, Writer wants.

Hence with no conflicts and/or confrontations, similarly.

Rudolph Kreutzer never performed the *Kreutzer* sonata.

this is not

One of the ennobling delights of Paradise, as promised by Thomas Aquinas:
Viewing the condemned as they are tortured and broiled below.

The friendship of Samuel Beckett and Alberto Giacometti.

Richard Strauss: Why do you have to write this way? You have talent.
Paul Hindemith: Herr Professor, you make your music and I'll make mine.

Porto d'Ercole. Where Caravaggio died.
Most probably of malaria.
In a tavern.

Georgia O'Keeffe died blind.

I saw *Hamlet, Prince of Denmark* played, but now the old plays begin to disgust this refined age.
Says John Evelyn's *Diary* for November 26, 1661.

With no social themes, i.e., no picture of society.

No depiction of contemporary manners and/or morals.

Categorically, with no politics.

Vulgar and dull, Ruskin dismissed Rembrandt as.
Brother to Dostoievsky, Malraux called him.

For whatever reason, Jean Sibelius did not write a note in the last thirty years of his life.

Kierkegaard died of a lung infection.
Or a disease of the spine.

Karl Barth's surmise:
That while the angels may play only Bach in praising God, among themselves they play Mozart.

Theophrastus pronounced that flute music could cure sciatica.
Not to mention epilepsy.

Alexander Pope died of dropsy.

John Milton died of gout.

Theophrastus said flute music would have cured that, also.

No one ever painted a woman's backside better than Boucher, said Renoir.

A novel entirely without symbols.

Robert of Naples: Giotto, if I were you, in this hot weather I would leave off painting for a while.
Giotto: So would I, assuredly—if I were you.

this is not

Matthew Arnold died of a heart attack while running for a streetcar in Liverpool.

Among Dickens' children:
Alfred Tennyson Dickens. Henry Fielding Dickens. Edward Bulwer-Lytton Dickens. Walter Landor Dickens. Sydney Smith Dickens.

Among Walt Whitman's brothers:
George Washington Whitman. Andrew Jackson Whitman. Thomas Jefferson Whitman.

Elizabeth I, visiting Cambridge University, delivered a lecture in Greek.
And then chatted less formally with students in Latin.

Thomas Mann died of phlebitis.

The likelihood that Anne Hathaway could not read.

Anne Hathaway.

The perhaps less than idle speculation that Columbus was a Jew.

Space is blue and birds fly through it.
Said Werner Heisenberg.

Ultimately, a work of art without even a subject, Writer wants.

There is no work of art without a subject, said Ortega.

A novel tells a story, said E. M. Forster.

If you can do it, it ain't bragging, said Dizzy Dean.

Xenocrates died after stumbling against a brass pot in the dark and cracking his skull.

Brunelleschi had a temporary restaurant and wine shop constructed in the highest reaches of the Florence cathedral while building his great cupola—so his workmen did not have to negotiate all that distance for lunch.

Maxim Gorky died of tuberculosis.
Or was he ordered murdered by Stalin?

Baudelaire died after being paralyzed and deprived of speech by syphilis.

I was tired and ill. I stood looking out across the fjord. The sun was setting. The clouds were colored red. Like blood. I felt as though a scream went through nature.
Said Edvard Munch.

Can only have been painted by a madman.
Said Munch of the same canvas.

Pico della Mirandola, not yet thirty-one, died of an unidentified fever.

William Butler Yeats died of heart failure.

The day of his death was a dark cold day.

Leigh Hunt once saw Charles Lamb kiss Chapman's Homer.
Henry Crabb Robinson once saw Coleridge kiss a Spinoza.

Lamb was in fact known to pretend surprise that people did not say grace before reading.

Horse Cave Creek, Ohio, Ambrose Bierce was born in.

Giorgione probably died of plague.

Ninon de Lenclos.

The solitary, melancholy life of Matthias Grünewald. Was he wholly sane?

Is Writer, thinking he can bring off what he has in mind?

And anticipating that he will have any readers?

There is only one person who has the right to criticize me, do you understand? And that is Picasso.
Said Matisse late in life.

Arthur Koestler was an enemy alien in solitary confinement in a London prison at the beginning of World War II when *Darkness at Noon* was published.

Pope Joan, a.k.a. John VII, 855–858.
Who died when taken by childbirth during a papal procession between St. Peter's and St. John Lateran.

There is no mention of writing in the *Iliad.* Any and all messages are passed along verbally.
Indicating incidentally that not one of the Greek warriors, during ten years at Troy, has ever sent a letter home.

Is John 8:6–8 the only place in the New Testament where Jesus is seen writing anything, if only marking on the ground with a finger?

The *Salon des Refusés.*

Le Déjeuner sur l'Herbe.

Joseph Conrad died of a heart seizure.

Does Writer even exist?

In a book without characters?

—And who are you? said he.—Don't puzzle me; said I. Says *Tristram Shandy* VII 33.

Hatred of the bourgeois is the beginning of all virtue, said Flaubert.

Tell all the Truth but tell it slant—

As a sort of mantra, Kant would sometimes recite a list of people who had lived long lives, hoping to match them. He reached eighty.

Gluck's face was pitted from smallpox.
Haydn's face was pitted from smallpox.
Mozart's face was pitted from smallpox.

Ludwig Wittgenstein died of prostate cancer.

My mind and fingers have worked like the damned. Homer, the Bible, Plato, Locke, Lamartine, Chateaubriand, Beethoven, Bach, Hummel, Mozart, Weber are all around me. I study them, I devour them with fury.
Wrote Liszt at twenty.

Obviously Writer exists.

Not being a character but the author, here.

Writer is *writing*, for heaven's sake.

Landscape of the Urinating Multitudes, Lorca called one of his New York poems.

Unmarried women should not bathe, said St. Jerome.
Ever. And should embrace the most deliberate squalor.
The less to breed temptation in the world.

Sappho was small and dark.
Though is made blond and fleshy by Raphael in his
Parnassus at the Vatican.

Horace was short and fat.
Admitting this himself in the *Satires*.

On the Knocking at the Gate in Macbeth.

Paul Celan's body was not found for eleven days after
he stepped off the Pont Mirabeau.
Nelly Sachs died on the day of his funeral. .

Only when Euripides was being performed would
Socrates go to the theater.

Rossini, on the *Symphony Fantastique:*
What a good thing it isn't music.

The Sabine farm.

Which is to say that Writer can even have headaches,
then?

Writer can have headaches.

this is not

Walter Scott frequently manufactured chapter epigraphs out of whole cloth, saying what he wished said, and then wrote in either *Old Play* or *Anon.* as the alleged source.

Paul Robeson died of pneumonia and kidney failure.

The King James Bible, the First Folio—both during James I.
Who on the other hand did not pay Chapman the royal stipend due on his translations.

According to Plutarch, Caesar was stabbed twenty-three times at his death.

Dvořák, to Sibelius: I have composed too much.
Brahms, to Dvořák: You do write a bit hastily.

Norman Mailer's sixth wife was the same age as his oldest daughter.

O, Time, Strength, Cash, and Patience!

Writer does have headaches.

In fact so did Virgil.

And Wordsworth.

Robert Lowell was in and out of mental institutions repeatedly.

Theodore Roethke was in and out of mental institutions repeatedly.

Roethke at least once taken in in handcuffs.

Madame Butterfly is set in Nagasaki.

And they so eagerly pressed towards the body, and so many daggers were hacking together, that they cut one another; Brutus, particularly, received a wound in his hand, and all of them were besmeared with blood.

Anna Akhmatova died after a series of heart attacks.

A grace to say before reading the *Oresteia*?
Before Kafka?

Wee Willie Keeler was five feet four and a half inches tall.

Balzac was five feet two.

Schubert was five one and a half.

Keats was less than five one.

A hyena that writes poetry on tombs, Nietzsche called Dante.

Martin Luther's own words, *re* the origin at Wittenberg Monastery of the key principles of the Protestant Reformation:

This knowledge the Holy Spirit gave me on the privy in the tower.

Anne Bradstreet died of what was then called consumption.

Sabrina fair,
Listen where thou art sitting
Under the glassy, cool, translucent wave.

Domenico Scarlatti was known to cross himself in veneration when taking about Handel's skill at the organ.

This is a portrait of Iris Clert if I say so.
Said Robert Rauschenberg in a telegram to a Paris art gallery.

Piero di Cosimo was found dead at the foot of a flight of stairs.

Hagia Sophia.

A woman named Mrs. Simon:
Who watched an elderly man on a train put his head out a window during an unrelenting November thunderstorm and hold it there for fully ten minutes.
And a year later at the Royal Academy came upon Turner's *Rain, Steam, and Speed* on exhibition.

Chi son? Chi son? Son un poeta.
Che cosa faccio? Scrivo.

Lavoisier was guillotined in the Reign of Terror.

The holy curiosity of enquiry, Einstein spoke of.

Paul Gauguin apparently died of a heart attack.

I pray you, give me leave to go from hence;
I am not well: send the deed after me,
And I will sign it.

When I saw a performance of this play at Drury Lane,
a beautiful pale-faced Englishwoman stood behind me in
the box and wept profusely at the end of the fourth act,
and called out repeatedly: The poor man is wronged.
    Wrote Heinrich Heine.

The assumption that Shylock is the merchant meant
by the title.

James Joyce and Isaac Babel were once guests at the
same dinner party.

E come vivo? Vivo.

This is a novel if Writer or Robert Rauschenberg says so.

Golder's Green, Sigmund Freud's ashes were buried at.
    In the Jewish cemetery where Conchita Supervia is also
buried.

18 this is not

Before the Normans brought *despair,* the Anglo-Saxon word was *wanhope.*

Edmund Wilson once punched Mary McCarthy in the face.

The frequent stags and deer in Lucas Cranach. Dogs barked when they saw them, someone said.
As birds flying into the cathedral at Seville were said to peck at the fruit in Murillo's *St. Anthony of Padua.*
Or other birds in an identical story about grapes in a panel by Zeuxis two millennia earlier.

Greater than any of us, Yeats called Rabindranath Tagore.

Descartes had an illegitimate daughter, named Francine, whom he loved dearly. And who died at five.

Wanhope.

Joan Sutherland's mezzo, Marilyn Horne was sometimes mindlessly pigeonholed as, early on.

Wagner insisted that Christ was not a Jew.
Though that Brahms was.

Murillo died after a fall from a scaffold.

Rudyard Kipling and Angela Thirkell were cousins.

I am going to drink myself dead, Modigliani made it known.

But died of tubercular meningitis.

Numerus clausus.

Ludwig Geyer.

And suddenly I realized that I should have to shoot the elephant after all. The people expected it of me and I had got to do it.

Gladstone read the *Iliad* thirty times.

Defoe, of the same opus:
A Ballad-Singer's Fable to get a Penny. All for the Rescue of a Whore.

Benny Goodman died of a heart attack while practicing Mozart.

Eleonora Duse died of pneumonia. In Pittsburgh.

There is no bay across from China, for the dawn to come up like thunder out of, anywhere near any road to Mandalay.

Cousin Ruddy.

I was twenty-five and he was sleeping with all the women, and at twenty-five you don't stand for that, even from a poet.

Said Marie Laurencin, of a breakup with Apollinaire.

This is even an epic poem, if Writer says so.
Requiring no one's corroboration.

Thomas Hardy was abusive to servants.
Tolstoy more so.

Toil, envy, want, the patron, and the jail. Being Samuel Johnson's précis of the poet's life.
Despondency and madness. Being Wordsworth's summation of the end of same.

Henry James once hid behind a tree to avoid having to spend time with Ford Madox Ford.

The actress in Dickens' life was Ellen Ternan, who was twenty-seven years younger than he. Dickens would leave her a thousand pounds in his will.

Virtually every home in Puritan America possessed a copy of *The Pilgrim's Progress*.

Let the father of the baby gather cherries for thee!

Bernini walked to the Gesù to pray every evening for forty years.

Cranmer watched Latimer and Ridley being burned at the stake no more than five months before he would be put to death in the same manner himself.

Head Tide, Maine, Edward Arlington Robinson was born in.

Cuchulain is illegitimate.
Arthur is illegitimate.
Gawain is illegitimate.
Roland is illegitimate.

What is this castle call'd that stands hard by?
They call it Agincourt.

The legend that Tycho Brahe died when his bladder burst after an interminable evening of drinking beer.

Djuna Barnes wrote in bed. Wearing makeup and with her hair done.
Edith Wharton wrote in bed. Scattering pages on the floor for a secretary to retrieve before typing.

Play the man, Master Ridley.

Hank Cinq.

Cavafy died of cancer of the larynx.

Pechorin.

Rarely, if ever, having had it come to mind:
That Marcel Proust constantly wheezed.

Did St. Augustine, who was asthmatic equally?

Ophir, from where gold and sandalwood and ivory and
apes and precious jewels and peacocks came. Which is
mentioned a dozen times in seven different books of the
Old Testament.
And which no one has ever discovered the location of.

Also even a sequence of cantos awaiting numbering, if
Writer says so.

Ingres spent fifteen years doing pencil portraits of
tourists in Rome.

> *The bomb in the bar will explode at thirteen-*
> *twenty.*

Cellini's narration of the casting of his *Perseus.*

The inexplicable logic by which Thackeray convinced
himself that Desdemona actually did have an affair with
Cassio.

Christopher Smart died mad. And in debtors' prison.

The Gesù, where St. Ignatius Loyola is buried. Bernini's
unimpeachable piety—

Yet the indisputable insinuation of orgasm in his *Ecstasy of St. Teresa.*

Romain Rolland died of tuberculosis.

Sigrid Undset died of a stroke.

The friendship of Heine and Karl Marx.

Claude Lévi-Strauss, Maurice Merleau-Ponty, and Simone de Beauvoir were once teachers in the same *lycée.*

The greatest lyric poet Germany ever knew, Gottfried Benn called Else Lasker-Schüler.
Who at sixty-four was beaten with an iron pipe by young Nazis on a street in Berlin.

Marianne Moore once read a book on the craft of pitching by Christy Mathewson.

The apparent evidence that Lawrence Durrell committed incest with one of his daughters. Who eventually killed herself.

Lady Mary Wortley Montagu died of breast cancer.

La vida de Lazarillo de Tormes.

this is not

I cannot endure to read a line of poetry; I have tried lately to read Shakespeare, and found it so intolerably dull that it nauseated me.

Says Darwin's *Autobiography.*

It is Arnaut Daniel, in *Purgatorio* XXVI, who was the original *miglior fabbro.*

Byron knew no music.
Pope knew no music.
Johnson knew no music and very little of art, either.

Ernest Hemingway once challenged Hugh Casey to a boxing match. Casey knocked Hemingway down repeatedly.

Hemingway kicked Casey in the groin.

On an ancient sundial in Ibiza: *Ultima multis.*
The last day for many.

Fayaway.

Much of what we have of Aristotle was not strictly speaking written by Aristotle at all. But would appear to be classroom notes taken down by others.

Both of Verdi's parents were illiterate.
Like Abraham Lincoln's.

Elegies to the Spanish Republic.

From Herodotus, on Thermopylae:
It chanced that at this time the Lacedaemonians held the outer guard and were seen by the spy. Some of them engaged in gymnastic exercises, others were combing their long hair. At this the spy greatly marveled.

The Spartans on the sea-wet rock
Sat down and combed their hair.

Roman Jakobson, when Mayakovsky once read him his newest poems:
Very good. But not as good as Mayakovsky.

For that matter Writer also has backaches.

As did Shelley.

A poet is a waste-good and an unthrift, in that he is born to make the taverns rich and himself a beggar.
Said Robert Greene.

But to speak plainly, I think him an honest man.
Greene also said.

One of Robert Frost's daughters went insane.
One of his sons killed himself.

Christopher Marlowe, a stage direction:
The Pope crosses himself, and Faustus hits him a box on the ear.

Puccini, sipping coffee, once told Lucrezia Bori that her costume was too neat for the last act of *Manon Lescaut,* in which Manon is destitute.

And dumped the coffee on her gown.

Verses of Propertius were found copied out on walls in Pompeii.

The seemingly authentic report that a doctor performed an autopsy on the Abbé Prévost after a stroke— to discover that only the autopsy had killed him.

He who wrote that painting is a higher art than sculpture was as ignorant as a maidservant, said Michelangelo.

Meaning Leonardo.

Chopin died of tuberculosis.

Salvador Dali once gave a lecture in London while wearing a diving helmet.

And nearly suffocated.

Thomas Gainsborough, while painting Sarah Siddons: Damn your nose, madame! There's no end to it.

Katherine Anne Porter died of Alzheimer's disease.

Palestrina's tomb, once in St. Peter's, for obscure reasons no longer exists.

Musicae Princeps, it had said. Prince of music.

Would Emily Dickinson have been aware that Lord Jeffrey Amherst arranged for blankets infected with small-pox to be set out for ill-clothed Indians to come upon during the French and Indian War?

The case for William Davenant having been Shakespeare's illegitimate son.

A Novel Without a Hero. Being the subtitle of *Vanity Fair.*
Though there, at least in part, meaning only that the book has a heroine instead.

Catullus once wrote a poem criticizing Caesar.
And was invited to dinner.

Osip Mandelstam once wrote a poem criticizing Stalin.
And died in the gulag.

Martin Heidegger, in 1933:
The Führer, and he alone, is the sole German reality and law, today and in the future.

Henry Miller died of cardiovascular failure.

B. Traven died of prostate cancer and sclerosis of the kidneys.

If Stephen Crane had in fact lived on an additional forty-plus years, how different might the hierarchy of American letters have been in that period?

No water-drinker ever wrote a poem that lasted.
Says Horace in the *Epistles*.

Un livre, c'est la mort d'un arbre.
Said St.-John Perse.

If you find this work difficult, and wearisome to follow, take pity on me, for I have repeated these calculations seventy times.
Wrote Johannes Kepler.

Italo Calvino died of a cerebral hemorrhage.

There is no description of Helen's beauty anywhere in the *Iliad*.
Strangely like is she to some deathless goddess to look upon, being all that is said.
Though the Trojan elders do acknowledge that no one could be blamed for having endured a war because of her.

Calderón de la Barca was once arrested for molesting nuns.

The John Dryden translation of Plutarch's *Lives*, eternally in print.
Which Dryden evidently did not do, but farmed out.

A face to lose youth for, to occupy age
With the dream of.

The speculation in later antiquity that Euripides had had two wives at the same time.

Life consists in what a man is thinking of all day, Emerson said.

Jean-Paul Sartre played the piano.
George Eliot played the piano.
André Gide played the piano.

The painting has a life of its own, said Jackson Pollock.

Henri Bergson died of pulmonary congestion.

Paul Klee played the violin.
Matisse played the violin.
Jeremy Bentham played the violin, the harpsichord, and the organ.

Schopenhauer was found dead sitting at his breakfast.

All your better deeds / Shall be in water writ, wrote Beaumont and Fletcher, two hundred years before Keats.
Teach me to heare Mermaides singing, wrote Donne, three hundred years before Eliot.

Marie Antoinette sat for twenty portraits by Vigée-Lebrun.

Anne Boleyn played the lute, the harp, the flute, and the rebec. And sang.

Voltaire, in an amiable mood about Jews:
A brigand people, atrocious, loathsome, whose law is the law of savages, and whose history is a tissue of crimes against humanity.

If you will it, it is no dream.
Said Theodor Herzl.

The word *Bible* never appears in Shakespeare. Jesus Christ is mentioned eleven times.

Cy Young died of a heart attack.

Lou Stevenson, Robert Louis was commonly called.

Dante quotes *The Consolation of Philosophy*.
Chaucer quotes *The Consolation of Philosophy*.
Milton quotes *The Consolation of Philosophy*.

What is Hamlet reading, in Act II Scene ii, when Polonius inquires and Hamlet says Words, words, words?

Polybius died after a fall from a horse.
At eighty-two.

Anacreon choked to death on a grape seed.
At eighty-five.

Walter Scott walked with a limp from childhood polio.

The apparently never to be resolved question of whether it was Byron's left foot that was crippled, or his right.

Edmund Wilson and a young Lionel Trilling once made use of adjacent urinals in a men's room at the New School for Social Research. Trilling was thrilled when Wilson indicated familiarity with some of his work.
What tall building could who have shouted this from, that Writer knows it all these decades later?

St. Teresa of Ávila played the tambourine.

F. Scott Fitzgerald's spelling:
Ullyses.

John Galsworthy died of a brain tumor.

Could Richard the Lion-Hearted speak English?

The traveler with nothing in his pockets whistles indifferently as he strolls past the thief.
Says Juvenal X.

Kant kept a portrait of Rousseau on the wall of his study.
Tolstoy, as a student, wore a medallion portrait of him instead of his Orthodox cross.

His usylessly unreadable Blue Book of Eccles.

Heinrich Schliemann died after collapsing with an unidentified fever on a street in Naples.

George Gissing died of pneumonia.

Watching Edmund Kean. Like reading Shakespeare by flashes of lightning, Coleridge said.

Donatello, at work on his *Zuccone,* heard muttering at the stone:
Speak, damn you, talk to me.

Pope Clement XIV, on Houdon's *St. Bruno:*
That saint would talk, were it not that the rules of his order impose silence.

I gotta use words when I talk to you.

And Sir Launcelot awoke, and went and took his horse, and rode all that day and all night in a forest, weeping.

Sherwood Anderson died of peritonitis after swallowing a toothpick.

Remembering only belatedly *re* Houdon:
That the Jefferson on the American nickel and the Washington on the quarter are from likenesses of his, also.

For as long as a millennium, until well into the Middle Ages, Menander was the most widely quoted author in Western literature outside of Homer.

The greatest lesbian poet since Sappho, Auden called Rilke.

Teaching, Lilli Lehmann actually tied Geraldine Farrar's hands behind her back to keep her from gesticulating.
And once threw a book at Olive Fremstad.

Was Moses an Egyptian?
As Manetho insisted twenty-two hundred years before Freud?

Fremstad. Who herself would later even visit a morgue to test the weight of an actual severed head before singing *Salome*.

A granddaughter of Wagner's worked as a waitress at Schrafft's in New York City during World War II.

Dinner at Benjamin Robert Haydon's studio, St. John's Wood, December 28, 1817:
Haydon. John Keats. Charles Lamb (drunk). William Wordsworth.

this is not

Gaily bedight,
A gallant knight
In sunshine and in shadow . . .

Patched together from pieces filched here and there, Beethoven jestingly scribbled on the manuscript of the C-sharp Minor Quartet.
Affording his publisher a fit.

Leonardo is a bore, according to Renoir.

My cook knows more about counterpoint, said Handel the first time he heard Gluck.

Let us go closer to the fire and see what we are saying.

Thomas Girtin, who was dead of tuberculosis at twenty-seven:
Had he lived I should have starved, said Turner.

Flaubert died of what was then called apoplexy, i.e., presumably a stroke.

If its length is not considered a merit it has no other, said Edmund Waller of *Paradise Lost.*

Thomas Hardy wrote a carefully sanitized third-person biography of himself and left it behind for his widow to pretend she was the author of.

Not a soul to talk to about Bloom. Lent the chapter to one or two people but they know as much about it as the parliamentary side of my arse.

Wrote Joyce to Frank Budgen.

Sarah Bernhardt was known to sleep in an open coffin.

Pope offended so many people with the *Dunciad* that he subsequently never left home without pistols.

Or his Great Dane.

Philip Larkin died of cancer of the esophagus.

Only hours afterward, a twenty-five-volume diary that he had kept for almost fifty years was destroyed by one of his executors.

Less of a loss, Writer assumes, than the then-current last volume of Sylvia Plath's that was destroyed by Ted Hughes.

Or the burning of Byron's *Memoirs*.

> *Had journeyed long,*
> *Singing a song,*
> *In search of El Dorado.*

This is even a mural of sorts, if Writer says so.

Marco Polo dictated the narrative of his travels to a fellow prisoner while in a jail in Genoa.

this is not

Jorge Luis Borges married a second wife at eighty-six.
John Dewey married a second wife at eighty-eight.

If it is just food you want, you will find that, she said in
a voice calm, a little deep, quite cold.

Eugene O'Neill died of bronchial pneumonia in a
Boston hotel room.

Albrecht Dürer died of malaria.

Sure I posed. I was hungry.

Caesar's corpse lay at the Senate for some hours before
slaves finally bore it away on a litter.
With one arm hanging down, Suetonius makes note of.

Enrico Caruso died of a minor pleural infection that
became fatal only after an Italian physician evidently used
an unsterilized instrument in examining him.

. Xanadu. Kubla Khan. Writer's tendency to misremem-
ber that they actually did exist.

Rustichello.

Opera bored me.
Said Helen Traubel.

Nobody knows the Traubel I've seen.
Said Rudolf Bing.

Jean Harlow died of cerebral edema brought on by uremic poisoning.

The friendship of Claude Monet and Georges Clemenceau.

Schubert could never afford a piano.

February 18, 1564. Michelangelo dies in Rome.
February 18, 1564. Galileo is born in Pisa.

Shakespeare is born that same year.

Isaac Newton is born the year Galileo dies.

The Amelia Curran portrait of Shelley, which has *been* Shelley since it was first reproduced via engraving in 1833.
But which was considered so unlifelike that Mary Shelley always intended to throw it out.

Galileo played the lute.

An Irish smut-dealer, Anthony Comstock called George Bernard Shaw.

This was Mr Bleaney's room.

this is not

Einstein died of an abdominal aneurysm. Which one of his doctors said was the result of tertiary syphilis.

Caspar David Friedrich.

Diego Rivera very rarely bathed.
Said Lupe Marin, the second of his four wives.

Roger Bacon probably did not invent gunpowder.

Alexander the Great was once pontificating about art in Apelles' studio. Apelles suggested that he change the subject—it being less than appropriate for the young apprentices to be tittering behind his back.

Ayot St. Lawrence.

The Delaware River, Einstein's ashes were scattered in.

My son, think of the future! With genius, one may die. With money, one can eat.
Said Cézanne's father.

No pasarán!

John Millington Synge died of lymph cancer.

Alexander also once commissioned Apelles to paint one of his mistresses, named Campaspe. Apelles fell in love with her. Alexander gave her to the artist.

Festina lente: Celerity should be contempered with cunctation.

Said Sir Thomas Browne.

Gustav Mahler's father was a tavernkeeper.

Ivan Goncharov was essentially deranged in the last thirty years of his life.

And insisted that every word Turgenev published had been stolen from him.

Following the Restoration, Cromwell's body was disinterred and hanged from a gibbet.

After his death in battle, Zwingli's body was mutilated and burned on a heap of dung.

And the sister of Tubal-cain was Naamah.

Rossini said he wept, the first time he heard Paganini.

Josephus says that practically every subsequent ancient historian thought of Herodotus as a liar.

Geoffrey of Monmouth was called a shameless liar in his own lifetime.

Thomas Otway died destitute.

Dimitri Mitropoulos died of a heart attack while conducting at La Scala.

this is not

The death of Patroclus, *Iliad* XVI:
Even as he spoke, the shadow of death came over him.
His soul fled from his limbs and went down to the house
of Hades, bemoaning its fate, leaving manhood and youth.

The death of Hector, *Iliad* XXII:
Even as he spoke, the shadow of death came over him.
His soul fled from his limbs and went down to the house
of Hades, bemoaning its fate, leaving manhood and youth.

The word *synagogue* is actually Greek.
And originally meant a Christian assembly.

Minyan.

There was a large rock near. She hurled her head at the
stone, so that she broke her skull and was dead.
Says the earliest version of *Deirdre of the Sorrows.*

John Lyly's sonnet on Apelles and Campaspe.
The Tiepolo fresco showing Apelles painting her.

The semiliterary, semicolloquial, often tin-eared and
generally annoying prose of H. L. Mencken.

Benjamin Britten died of a heart condition.

Aaron Copland died of respiratory failure brought on by
pneumonia.

Virtually beyond Writer's imagining:
The lost *eighty* or so plays, each, of Aeschylus and Euripides.
The lost *one hundred and ten* of Sophocles.

Tobias Smollett died of tuberculosis.

Botticelli seems to have signed only one painting in his life.

Simple Wordsworth and his childish verse, Byron called him and it.

Sartre's father was a naval officer.
Lytton Strachey's father was a general.

Flann O'Brien, on Brendan Behan:
A lout.

Congreve wrote *The Way of the World* at thirty. And lived twenty-nine more years without writing one further word for the stage.

Nikos Kazantzakis once spent two years as a contemplative on Mount Athos.

> *Like a long-legged fly upon the stream*
> *His mind moves upon silence.*

this is not

Nietzsche, on George Sand:
A writing cow.

Thomas Hobbes was once Francis Bacon's secretary.
Andrew Marvell was once John Milton's.

In whatever version of the legend, Galahad is unvary-
ingly established as a direct descendant of Joseph of Ari-
mathea.
Ergo as Jewish.
Perceval likewise.

Was Lorenzo Ghiberti the first artist of consequence to
write an autobiography?

A friend, when Oliver Goldsmith briefly practiced medicine in London:
Kindly prescribe only for your enemies.

Louise Homer died of coronary thrombosis.

Matisse: In modern art, it is indubitably to Cézanne
that I owe the most.
Picasso: He was my one and only master. Cézanne! It
was the same with all of us—he was like our father.

Aeschylus never saw the Parthenon.

Zora Neale Hurston died in a welfare home.
And was buried in an unmarked grave.

André Malraux died from a blood clot on his lung.

On principle, Bertrand Russell gave away all of his considerable inherited wealth in his late twenties. And earned his own way thereafter.

Wagner was five months older than Verdi.
Wittgenstein was five months older Heidegger.

Elizabeth Barrett was six years older than Browning.

Mont Sainte-Victoire.

Enrique Grenados drowned while attempting to save his wife when their ship was torpedoed by a German submarine in the English Channel in World War I.

Pyrrhus died after being struck by a tile flung from a roof.

Hit Sign Win Suit.

Whitman said he had read *The Heart of Midlothian* a dozen or more times.

Among Wittgenstein's spellings, when using English: Anoied. Realy. Excelentely. Expences. Affraid. Cann't.

this is not

Plotinus did not begin to write until he was fifty.

Goethe was seventy-eight before he started Part II of *Faust*.

Two millennia before Princess Diana, Virgil, visiting Rome, would be forced to flee even into the private homes of strangers because of admirers crowding after him on the streets.

And this when he had written only the *Eclogues* and the *Georgics*, the *Aeneid* to be posthumous.

I had but a glimpse of Virgil, Ovid himself, younger, had to say.

Fulke Greville was murdered by a disaffected servant.

Asculum.

Fallen by a beldam's hand in Argos.

Account for Hamlet's treatment of Ophelia.

Walter Johnson died of a brain tumor.

For we must consider that we shall be as a city on a hill.

Lice, Dickens labeled critics.
Swine, D. H. Lawrence preferred.

Samuel Barber was Louise Homer's nephew.

Southwell was hanged and then drawn and quartered at Tyburn.

Palestrina's *Stabat Mater.*
Pergolesi's.

Without fail, given pause at recalling that Captain Ahab is a Quaker.

As similarly always needing a moment for the precise meaning of *drawn and quartered* to register.

Paracelsus may have died after a brawl in a tavern.

And his sandal shoon.

Gerhart Hauptmann was a supporter of the Nazis.
Igor Stravinsky admired Mussolini.

Stabat Mater dolorosa
Iuxta crucem lacrimosa

Vivaldi's. Haydn's. Rossini's.
Poulenc's.

The legend that Gregory the Great had to be dragged to St. Peter's by main force, when he was elected Pope.

No man will ever write a better tragedy than *Lear,* Shaw said.

this is not

The Burning Babe.

Orson Welles died of a heart attack.

Stephen Foster never learned which side won the Civil War.

Michelangelo. Piero di Cosimo. Guido Reni. Pontormo. Tintoretto.
All of whom wanted no one anywhere near them when working.
Piero and Pontormo becoming pathological about it.

Jacopone da Todi.

Anna Pavlova died of pneumonia.

Ronald Firbank died of pneumonia.

The little Marcel, Proust was called. All his life.

A. E. Housman, on the surest source of poetic inspiration:
A pint, at luncheon.

Kirsten Flagstad, on the most critical aspect of singing Wagner:
Comfortable shoes.

Les Saltimbanques, which inspired the fifth of the *Duino Elegies:*

Rilke in fact having been a guest in a home in Munich where the canvas hung above his desk for months.

Anthony Trollope wrote seven pages a day, seven days a week.
And would actually begin a new book if he came to the end of one before his day's quota had been met.

Cry you mercy, I took you for a joint stool.

Eliot's first wife, Vivien, insisted upon washing her own bedsheets.
Even when staying at a hotel.

My breviary, Montaigne referred to Plutarch as.
While frequently quoting him with no acknowledgment whatsoever.

Which Seneca had also long since made a practice of.

Sinclair Lewis died of a heart attack.

Thomas Eakins was once fired for removing a loincloth from a male model in a women's life-drawing class in Philadelphia.

Defoe's father was a butcher.

Sadi. Rumi. Hafiz.

Saul of Tarsus very likely participated in the stoning of St. Stephen.

Was he also an epileptic?

Was John the Baptist an Essene?

I was, with God's help, born poor.

Ralph Ellison died of pancreatic cancer.

Tarsus. Being also where Cleopatra arrives, on her barge, to meet Mark Antony.

On the river Cydnus.

In Turkey.

Tommaso Campanella spent twenty-seven years in a papal dungeon for heresy.

An information bureau of the human condition, Theodor Adorno called Kafka.

Shelley, at nineteen, was sent down from Oxford for publishing a pamphlet on atheism.

Landor, at the same age, was expelled for shooting a fellow student in a political argument.

Two hundred and forty-three people die in the *Iliad* who are named by name.

One hundred and forty-seven *separate* wounds are mentioned.

The Graham Sutherland portrait of Winston Churchill.
Which Clementine Churchill cut into pieces and then
burned.

Exsultate, Jubilate. K 165.
Maria Stader.

Writer's tendency to forget that there were two other
Brontë sisters, scarcely older, who died when Charlotte
and Emily and Anne were eight and six and four.
Consumptive, the brood.

Boris Pasternak evidently died of lung cancer that had
spread to the area of his heart.

Peredelkino.

I have never heard of any old man forgetting where he
had hidden his money, Cicero said.

Self-Portrait in a Convex Mirror:
1524, Parmigianino's version dating from.

Philip of Macedon: If I reach Lacedaemon, not one
stone will I leave upon another.
The Spartans: If.

Enrico Fermi died of stomach cancer.

John von Neumann died of cancer of the brain.

this is not

Haworth Parsonage.

Shakespeare's Sonnets / Never Before Imprinted. A
small quarto, 1609:
Sixpence.

> *But on a May morwening upon Malverne hilles*
> *Me befel a ferly, of fairye me thoughte.*

Jenny Lind died in the Malvern Hills.

My work is not a prize composition done to be heard
for the moment, but was designed to last forever.
Said Thucydides.

Pierre Bonnard and Wassily Kandinsky were near-
sighted.
As were Samuel Johnson and Tennyson.
And Nietzsche.

And Maria Callas.

Marshall McLuhan died of a stroke.

Robert Lowell once punched Jean Stafford in the face
and broke her nose.
Which he had broken two years earlier by drunkenly
smashing a car into a stone wall.

Men have died from time to time, and worms have
eaten them, but not for love.

Bach and Handel, born twenty-six days apart.
And never once meeting.

Beethoven was left-handed.

Rembrandt worked so slowly, especially in his later
years, that it became ever more difficult for him to find
sitters.
In good part explaining the hundred-odd self-portraits.

Luisa Tetrazzini died penniless.

Tolstoy, asked if he had read a recent play by Maurice
Maeterlinck:
Why should I? Have I committed a crime?

They who write ill, and they who ne'er durst wrote,
Turn critics out of mere revenge and spite.

—Said Dryden.

Ten censure wrong for one who writes amiss.

—Added Pope.

He was being called *Papa* Haydn well before he was
thirty.

Jacopo. Gentile. Giovanni.

Not to add sister Nicolosia, who married Andrea Mantegna.

Was Liszt the greatest pianist who ever lived?

Planning his *Balzac*, Rodin went so far as to search out a tailor the novelist had used forty years before—and had a suit made to the dead measurements.

Birgit Nilsson's debut at the Metropolitan Opera, as Isolde, was reviewed on the front page of the *New York Times*.

I am not overly fond of poetry and I do not read it willingly. In my reading, poems take up a very small space.
Said Ingeborg Bachmann.

Rodin died of pulmonary congestion.

Anabasis.

Your last novel was a flop. You've got two wonderful children depending on you. Don't you think it's time to consider doing something more financially responsible in your life?

This is also even an autobiography, if Writer says so.

Come away; poverty's catching. Wrote Aphra Behn.

Anni 68 Cenzza Ochiali, Canaletto signed a drawing in 1766.

At age sixty-eight, without spectacles.

Handel died blind.

Gaddo. Taddeo. Agnolo.
Lodovico. Agostino. Annibale.

Liszt sat down and played at sight what the rest of us toil over and in the end still get nowhere with, Clara Schumann said.

Or John Bellini, as Ruskin insisted on calling him.

Maria Malibran died at twenty-eight after being thrown from a horse.

Has time pardoned Paul Claudel?

Ruskin died of influenza.

Anton Webern was shot and killed by an American soldier in Austria at the end of World War II. Wholly by error.

There should be nothing in a novel that the author would not say out loud in the presence of a young girl, said William Dean Howells.

this is not

Kate Chopin died of what was apparently a brain hemorrhage.

Remind me to get some money from this bugger.

Piero della Francesca's father was a shoemaker.

Joseph Cornell lived with his mother all his life.

Admire the martyrs of Bloody Mary's reign.

D. H. Lawrence died of tuberculosis.

Charlotte Perkins Gilman was a niece of Harriet Beecher Stowe.

In his mid-twenties, Joseph Brodsky was sentenced to five years shoveling manure at the White Sea for what the Soviet Union saw as social parasitism.

Petrarch—and the St. Augustine eternally in his pocket.
Reading the *Confessions* at the peak of Mont Ventoux.

Romney painted Emma Hamilton nearly fifty times.

Clit lit.

Appointed *maestro di cappella* at St. Mark's in 1613, Monteverdi was robbed by highwaymen while moving there from Cremona.

Terence would appear to have died in a shipwreck.

The room was full of Sitwells. And Sacheverell others.

Jeanne Eagels died of an overdose of heroin.

Plutarch says Xerxes watched the debacle at Salamis from a golden throne on a hilltop above the strait—surrounded by scribes meant to record the trappings of a victory.

> *A king sate on the rocky brow*
> *Which looks o'er sea-born Salamis.*

Did Kierkegaard's father have venereal disease?

A good-natured man of principle.
Pablo Neruda called Stalin.

A saint and a martyr.
Ezra Pound called Hitler.

Mark Twain died of a heart condition.

Rupert Brooke's only brother died in World War I no more than weeks after Brooke himself.

Château-Thierry, La Fontaine was born in.

Realizing idly that every artist in history—until Writer's own century—rode horseback.

For instance Keats doing so beside the Tiber each morning until not long before his death.

George Sand, disdaining sidesaddle on a favorite mare she by chance called Colette.

Or twenty-three centuries earlier Pindar even reassuring readers that there would be horses in heaven.

I sprang to the stirrup, and Joris, and he;
I galloped, Dirck galloped, we galloped all three.

A monk asked Ts'ui-wei: For what purpose did the First Patriarch come from the West?
Ts'ui-wei answered: Pass me that chin rest.
As soon as the monk passed it, Ts'ui-wei thwacked him with it.

Any and all public gatherings were prohibited in Venice during a plague in 1576.
An edict that was unhesitatingly ignored at the death of Titian—so deserving was he felt to be of a state funeral.

To Helen. Poe was sixteen.
Le Bateau ivre. Rimbaud was sixteen.
Thanatopsis. Bryant was sixteen or seventeen.

Thomas Gray died of gout.

Jean Genet was a paid informer for the Nazis in World War II.

Colette the novelist died of cardiac arrest.

Salacious, bad-smelling, sick.
Said Van Wyck Brooks of Joyce.

While deriding Rimbaud as a neurasthenic little wretch.

Berlioz, on critics:
Where do they come from? At what age are they sent to the slaughterhouse?

Adam Mickiewicz died of cholera.

William Collins died mad.

Writer's equally idle realization that all of those same equestrian artificers likewise went through life without flush toilets.

What type of outhouse had Peter Paul Rubens, for example?

What bedroom slop bucket disguised as a clothes chest had Jane Austen?

this is not

Chaim Soutine died of stomach ulcers.

John Steinbeck died of a heart condition, little tempered by acute emphysema.

Kandinsky once invited Arnold Schoenberg to join the faculty at the Bauhaus.
Indicating magnanimously that while Jews were normally not welcome, an exception would here be made.

Oh! Celia, Celia, Celia shits!

This is the lamentable condition of our times, that men of art must seek alms of cormorants, and those that deserve best, be kept under by dunces.
Said Thomas Nashe in 1592.

For two decades, starting at twenty-five, Paul Valéry did not publish a line.

Wagner died in 1883.
Cosima not until 1930.

Dante Gabriel Rossetti died of Bright's disease.

Tennessee Williams choked to death on the plastic cap of a nasal spray.

Let's choose executors, and talk of wills.

He is either mad, or he is reading *Don Quixote*.
Said Philip III, at the sight of a student banging himself on the head and doubling over in hysterics over a book.

Perugino probably died of plague.

There is no one so foolish as to praise *Don Quixote*.
Said Lope de Vega.

The Metropolitan Museum's only Caravaggio, the early *Allegory of Music*, was not known of for more than three centuries.
And was walked off with for less than one hundred pounds when come upon in an English antique shop.

This can only be the devil or Bach himself!

No date will ever be available for Marian Anderson in Constitution Hall.
Said Constitution Hall.

Camus went through most of his adult life with recurrent tuberculosis.

Michael Tippett spent three months in Wormwood Scrubs as a conscientious objector in World War II.

The tail gunner on the *Enola Gay* wore a Brooklyn Dodgers cap.

Antonio Gaudí died after being hit by a streetcar in Barcelona.

Blaise Cendrars died after a series of strokes.

The worldwide influenza epidemic of 1918–1919 killed forty million people.
Including Apollinaire. And Egon Schiele.

And both of Mary McCarthy's parents.

Descartes and Pascal met twice.
Neither being impressed.

David Hume was grossly fat, reported even to crack chairs.
Edward Gibbon became equally so.
Amy Lowell as well.

What sort of chamber pot had Bishop Berkeley?

Enoch Arden.

The kind of person who is always somewhere else when the trigger is pulled, George Orwell described Auden as.

Orwell on Sean O'Casey:
Very stupid.

On Steinbeck:
Spurious.

La Trahison des clercs.

Until he was forty, Hermann Broch was the manager of his family's textile firm.

Grazia Deledda died of breast cancer.

Dost thou think Alexander look't o' this fashion i' th' earth? And smelt so? Pah!

Not even worth the trouble of condemning, said Gautier of Manet's *Olympia.*

As late as in 1874, Jacob Burckhardt felt licensed to dismiss Jan Vermeer as inconsequential:
Women reading and writing letters and such things.

Archilochos is said to have died in battle.

The most acute thinker ever born, Kant called Kepler.

The first English translation of *Madame Bovary* was done by a daughter of Karl Marx.
Who would later take her own life much the way Emma does.

this is not

An extant letter of Michelangelo's complains about money that Luca Signorelli borrowed and never repaid.

He was always strumming upon something—his hat, his watch fob, the table, the chair, as if they were the keyboard.
Said Constanze.

Far too many notes, my dear Mozart.

Quentin de La Tour died mad.

Charlie Parker died of pneumonia and a bleeding ulcer, though with unquestioned contributions from alcohol and drugs.

Quinquireme of Nineveh from distant Ophir.

Boccaccio's tale of Giotto, on horseback, caught in an August rainstorm.

Hunchback'd Papist, Pope was called in print.

Maeterlinck died of a heart condition.

Beethoven, preoccupied. Crossing to his washstand to pour water over his head oblivious of the fact that he is fully dresssed.

And even in the ages to come, men will make of us a song for telling.

Says Helen to Hector of their destiny.

Theodore Dreiser once tried to bribe H. L. Mencken to start a campaign promoting him for the Nobel Prize.

After the burning, Joan of Arc's remains were dumped into the Seine.

After the burning, Savonarola's remains were dumped into the Arno.

James Clerk Maxwell died of abdominal cancer.

During the thirty days' grace between his conviction and the hemlock, Socrates memorized a long poem by Stesichorus.

I wish to die knowing one thing more.

You have only to walk about until your legs are heavy, and then to lie down, and the poison will act.

Explains the jailer in *Phaedo.*

What Pieter Bruegel knew about summer.

Kipling, in Sussex, may have been the first author to actually dispense with horses, owning a motorcar as early as in 1902.

Henry Adams owned a Mercedes in France in 1904.

this is not

John Fletcher died of plague. Beaumont's death was apparently registered with no cause listed.

Trifles, Catullus waved away his verses as.
Two full thousand years ago.

The height of absurdity in serving up pure nonsense, or in stringing together senseless and extravagant masses of words, previously seen only in madhouses, was reached in Hegel.
Said Schopenhauer.

In or about December 1910 human character changed.

Yes, Virginia.

Ben Shahn was once an assistant to Diego Rivera.
Jackson Pollock was once an assistant to David Alfaro Siqueiros.

Richard Feynman's roommate, when they were both working at Los Alamos, was Klaus Fuchs.

Raymond Carver died of lung cancer.

Last Week I saw a Woman *flay'd*, and you will hardly believe, how much it altered her Person for the worse.

Why does there appear not to have been one word written about Jesus until he is mentioned by Josephus more than fifty years after his death?

Rembrandt's father was a corn miller.

Corot more than once added a few brushstrokes and then signed his own name to the work of other painters—who would otherwise not have been able to sell.

The St. Vincent de Paul of painting, he came to be called.

Ned Ludd was feeble-minded.

By far, the two greatest stylists who ever wrote in German were Heine and Nietzsche.

Said Nietzsche.

I painted this from myself. I was six-and-twenty years old. Albrecht Dürer. 1498.

Nancy Barron, a madwoman at the poorhouse farm in Concord.

Immortalized because Emerson could hear her endless screaming from his study.

Racine died of an abscess of the liver.

A bigot and a sot, Thomas Babington Macaulay called James Boswell.

Simone de Beauvoir died of pneumonia.

Giambattista Vico died of what sounds to have been Alzheimer's disease.

this is not

No great talent has ever existed without a tinge of madness, Seneca says Aristotle said.

All poets are mad, Robert Burton corroborated.

A fine madness, being how Michael Drayton read it in the case of Marlowe.

Gainsborough played the bass viol.

Laird of Auchinleck.

Written with the imagination of a drunken savage. Said Voltaire of *Hamlet*.

There is no foulness conceivable to the mind of man that has not been poured forth into its imbecile pages. Said Alfred Noyes of *Ulysses*.

Tom Macaulay, he was commonly called.

Jacques Offenbach died of a heart condition.

Jussi Bjoerling died of a heart condition.

Donatello kept extraordinary amounts of cash in a basket hung from the ceiling in his studio. Quite literally for his workmen or friends to take as they saw fit.

Seneca was a usurer.

*Ammannato, Ammannato, che bel marmo hai rov-
inato!*
What beautiful marble you have ruined. Said contemporary Florentines of his Neptune Fountain in the Piazza
della Signoria.

Nothing but a continued Heap of Riddles, Theobald
found in Donne.

And death i think is no parenthesis.

At least two people were drowned in the Seine because
of the crush along the route of Victor Hugo's funeral.

Antonello da Messina died of pleurisy.

The maniac who took a hammer to Michelangelo's
Pietà in 1972.
His counterpart who spray-painted *Kill Lies All* on the
Guernica in 1974.
The second of whom actually later owned an art gallery
in SoHo.

Knut Hamsun, at twenty-five, was told he had three
months to live because of rampant tuberculosis.
And died at ninety-three.

Oscar Wilde wrote *Salomé* in French.

En attendant Godot.

this is not

Lawrence Tibbett died after an automobile crash.

If it is art it is not for all, and if it is for all it is not art.
Said Schoenberg.

Three or four years after the Civil War, Thomas Carlyle
told the American Charles Eliot Norton that slavery
should be reinstituted.
Or that blacks should be eliminated altogether.

Starvation and/or massacre being obligingly suggested.

Durendal. Olifant.

A man must be a fool to deliberately stand up and be
shot at.
Said Hardy when he ceased writing novels after the
exorbitant denunciations of *Jude the Obscure.*

Andrea del Sarto's wife, Lucrezia.
Could she have conceivably for all the years been
misabused?

Elizabeth Bishop died of a cerebral aneurysm.

Elizabeth Bishop's mother died mad.

Lessing died of a stroke, though already wasted by
severe asthma and damaged lungs.

Plotinus died of what was probably throat cancer.

Rafael Sabatini's father was John McCormack's singing teacher.

An unforgotten lifetime debt of Writer's, since adolescence:
To Constance Garnett.

Half-cracked. Thomas Wentworth Higginson's earliest evaluation of Emily Dickinson.

Cyrano de Bergerac died in an accident involving a falling beam.

Mitsubishi manufactured the torpedoes used at Pearl Harbor.
Porsche manufactured tanks.

O the Chimneys.

Robert Browning died of a heart attack.

This is also a continued heap of riddles, if Writer says so.

Simplify, simplify.

For a time, Rossetti, Swinburne, and George Meredith shared a house in Chelsea.

For a time, Domenichino, Guido Reni, and Francesco Albani roomed together in Rome.

The latter three later despising each other.

Whenever possible, Erasmus sought out Jewish physicians.

Whenever possible, Montaigne sought out Jewish physicians.

Rubens died of arteriosclerosis.

Orwell died of tuberculosis.

Kathleen Mavourneen.

Artemisia Gentileschi. Agostino Tassi.

Sir Thomas Wyatt died of an undiagnosed fever.

Heine died of the spinal paralysis, presumably syphilitic, that had confined him to what he referred to as his *mattress-tomb* for his last eight years.

Archaeological evidence for the historical reality of Theseus.

Didier. Férol. Langlois.

The next shot went into a brain which was already dead.

Vicente Huidobro died of a stroke.

Did Ben Jonson have any notion that Drummond of Hawthornden was writing all that down?

Darling, you'll never guess what happened in the men's room at the New School for Social Research tonight!
Oh, dear. Not all the way down the inside of your pants leg again?

It is not necessary to have dandruff to be a genius, Puccini said.

I started walking home across the bridge.

Beethoven, Gluck, Schubert, and Brahms are buried in the same Vienna cemetery.
Emerson, Hawthorne, and Thoreau are buried in the same one in Concord.

Isaac Bashevis Singer's father was a rabbi.

Marc Chagall was the grandson of a *shohet*.

Braque, an image of Picasso at the moment of *Les Demoiselles d'Avignon:*
Drinking turpentine and spitting fire.

Writer reminding himself that the Avignon here was a brothel in Barcelona, not the city.

What artists do cannot be called work.
Says Flaubert's *Dictionary of Accepted Ideas*.

La Grosse Margot.

The precious, pinchbeck, ultimately often flat prose of
Vladimir Nabokov.
The fundamentally uninteresting sum total of his work.

Some dozen years after *Berlin Alexanderplatz*, living
on handouts as a wartime refugee in California, Alfred
Doeblin applied for a Guggenheim Fellowship. With a
recommendation from Thomas Mann.
   Guess.

The friendship of Lorca and Salvador Dali.

   It may be for years, and it may be forever.

Or even a polyphonic opera of a kind, if Writer says that
too.

   André Chénier had published only two poems when he
was guillotined.

   Skeptic: And can you possibly have read all these walls
of books?
   Anatole France: Not one tenth of them. I don't suppose
you use your Sèvres china every day?

Gabriele Münter.

Lise Meitner.

Prokofiev died on the same day as Stalin.

Aldous Huxley died on the same day as John F. Kennedy.

Nathanael West died one day after F. Scott Fitzgerald.

Hemingway died one day after Louis-Ferdinand Céline.

West and Fitzgerald had had dinner together one week earlier.

Machado de Assis was an epileptic.

Twice as many baseball batters are hit by a pitch on days when the temperature is in the nineties as when it is in the seventies.

Rousseau was categorically convinced of the existence of vampires.

Gammer Gurton's Needle.

Goldengrove unleaving.

It took Eliot forty years to allow that the word *Jew* in *Gerontion* might be capitalized.

Then Abraham fell upon his face and laughed.

June 16, 1904.
Stephen Dedalus has not had a bath since October 1903.

Transnistria.

Edward Teller lost a foot in a streetcar accident.

Pär Lagerkvist died of a stroke.

Howells and Mark Twain once canceled a dinner they had planned for Maxim Gorky—after discovering that the woman he had sailed from Russia with was not his wife.

Fra Angelico was said not to be able to paint a Christ without weeping.

For the World, I count it not an Inne, but an Hospitall; and a place not to live, but to Dye in.
Says Browne in the *Religio Medici.*

Cola di Rienzi's father was a saloonkeeper.

Django Reinhardt spent his childhood in a Gypsy caravan.
And was considerably less than literate.

César Vallejo died of an intestinal infection.

I've been reading *Cousin Bette*. I've been reading it all
summer. I may never finish.

William Kapell died in a plane crash.

Dinu Lipatti died of lymphogranulomatosis.

Archytas, who invented the baby's rattle.
Which Aristotle actually takes note of. In *Politics* VIII
6, 1340b 25–28.

Chekhov died of consumption.

Karl Ditters von Dittersdorf at least once played the
violin in a string quartet in which two of the other per-
formers were Mozart and Haydn.

Beaumarchais died of a stroke.

Alain-Fournier was killed in action in France less than
two months into World War I.

Protesilaus, in *Iliad* II. The first Greek to leap from the
ships onto Trojan soil.
And the first slain.

Pylaemenes. Who is fatally speared at the collarbone by
Menelaus in *Iliad* V.
And is inadvertently shown alive again in *Iliad* XIII.

He fell, immortal in a bulletin.

this is not

East Tenth Street in Manhattan, Adelina Patti grew up on.

There is no hippopotamus in this lecture room at the present moment.

Lamarck died blind.
And was buried in a pauper's grave.

Gehenna.

Isaac Newton died of complications from a kidney stone.

Ramanujan died of tuberculosis.

Badges? I don't have to show you no stinkin' badges.

One of St. Jerome's letters to St. Augustine took nine years to be delivered.

Capitoline. Palatine. Aventine. Caelian. Esquiline. Viminal. Quirinal.

What existed before the Big Bang?
Where?
Exclude God from your response.

Camille Pissarro was poverty-stricken for much of his working career.
Alfred Sisley was perhaps worse off, and for longer.

William Goyen died of leukemia.

Fragonard's *The Swing.*
Which William Carlos Williams had the impression
was Watteau's.

Plato talked too much, Diogenes said.
While dismissing Socrates as a lunatic altogether.

Erasmus was indisputably the most famous author of
his day. Thomas More even admitted to being thrilled
that the very fact of their friendship would help keep his
own name alive with posterity.

A piece of *dreck,* Luther on the other hand called him.

I, O Plato, see a table and a cup. But I see no tableness
or cupness.

Dickens' astonishing manic walks. Of as many as
twenty-five miles—and at a headlong pace.

Oedipus Rex did not win first prize in the dramatic
competition in the year when it was first presented.

Any contemporary philosopher who ventured to com-
pare himself with Leibniz could at best wind up wishing
he had a quiet corner to go die in, said Diderot.

William Wycherley married a second wife, far younger than he, at seventy-five.
And died eleven days later.

George Herbert died of consumption.

The most odious of small creeping things, Landor called critics.

A *walk*? What on earth *for*?
Asked Auden at someone's country home.

Dizzy Dean had less than a fourth-grade education.
But a post-doctoral sense of the joys of that game, said Marianne Moore.

Hemingway, on Ezra Pound's indictment for treason:
If Ezra has any sense he should shoot himself. Personally I think he should have shot himself somewhere along after the twelfth canto although maybe earlier.

Disraeli said he had read *Pride and Prejudice* at least sixteen times.

The straight line predominates in nature.
Ingres once said.

Only curved lines are to be found in nature.
Ingres once said.

Maud Gonne was six feet tall.
Akhmatova was five feet eleven.

Jessica Mitford died of brain cancer.

Ellen Glasgow was buried in the same coffin as the exhumed remains of her two favorite dogs.

Venus Pudica. Venus Anadyomene.

Absolute reason expired at eleven o'clock last night.

> *Think how many royal bones*
> *Sleep within this heap of stones.*

—Wrote Beaumont *re* Westminster Abbey.

Roger Martin du Gard died of a heart condition.

Arthur Honegger died of a heart condition.

Henry James ill-advisedly took an author's curtain call on the opening night of his play *Guy Domville*.
And was hissed.

The Hebrew in Exodus 34:29–30 translates literally to say that after Moses came down from Sinai for the second time, the skin on his face sent forth beams, meaning it shone.

A mistranslation in the Latin Vulgate said he was horned.

Ergo Michelangelo. And cetera.

Rameau died of typhoid fever.

Lovis Corinth.

Rilke wrote standing up.
Lewis Carroll wrote standing up.
Thomas Wolfe wrote standing up.

Robert Lowell and Truman Capote wrote lying down.

Writer sits.

Jens Peter Jacobsen died of tuberculosis.

Balzac often worked for sixteen or eighteen hours consecutively, generally beginning at midnight.

Awash in coffee.

Gibbon died of infectious complications from hydrocele.

Contemporary architecture is basically a bore.

Writer sometimes also talks to himself.

As did Yeats.

As did Yeats even walking the streets of Dublin.

Mad as the mist and snow.

Writer sitting and/or talking to himself being no more than renewed verification that he exists.

In a book without characters.

As noted, not being a character but the author, here.

We are and we are not.
Said Heraclitus.

Even with innumerable obvious likes and/or dislikes and certain self-evident preoccupations.

How frequently was *Anon.* a woman?

Marcel Duchamp died of prostate cancer.

Already condemned by lung cancer, Duke Ellington died of pneumonia.

The word *ghetto* originally meant foundry.
Until the Jews of Venice were forced to live on an island that had previously been the site of one.

Knowledge is not intelligence.
Heraclitus additionally said.

Thales, solving the height of the pyramids:
Simply by measuring their shadows precisely when his own shadow matched his height.

The legend that as a young man Leonardo was so strong he could straighten a horseshoe with his bare hands.

Robert Capa was killed by a land mine in Vietnam.

Fray Luis de Léon, returning to his Salamanca classroom after five years of imprisonment by the Inquisition:
As I was saying . . .

Hey, Dad, hot this for me, please?

A tavern chair is the throne of human felicity, Johnson said.

Disgusting eating habits, there or elsewhere, Boswell says Johnson had.

Roald Dahl died of leukemia.

There can be no doubt that there is something peculiar in the condition of the English retina.
Said Taine, viewing a first exhibition of Pre-Raphaelite art.

I hear a white horse on the way.

G. K. Chesterton died of heart failure.

Hilaire Belloc died, senile, at eighty-three, when he set his clothing on fire by spilling coal from a grate.

Hardy's father was a stonemason.

Turner's mother died mad.

Chadds Ford, Pennsylvania.

On radio, the opening lines of Verlaine's *Chanson d'automne:*
Being the signal to the European underground that the D-Day invasion was underway.

Jane! Jane! Jane!

Filippo Lippi died of quinsy.

Account for Joan of Arc.

According to Vasari, ordinary citizens in Florence were so impressed by a Madonna of Cimabue's that it was actually carried in a procession from his workshop to Santa Trinita.
Heralded by trumpets.

It is an aspect of probability that many improbable things will happen.

this is not

Aristotle says Agathon said.

A likely impossibility is always preferable to an unconvincing possibility.
Aristotle himself added, *re* tragedy.

Wittgenstein had nephews fighting on both sides in World War II.

Meyerhold was executed by the Soviets.

He dug a grave of the same length as Pakhom's form from head to heels—three Russian ells—and buried him.

Rubén Darío died of cirrhosis of the liver.

Diderot died of coronary thrombosis while sitting at dinner.

I used to say to them, Go boldly in among the English, and then I used to go boldly in myself.
Said Joan.

He could not get rid of the idea that he was damned, and he would have drowned himself if he had not been prevented by force.
Says a chronicle from the monastery where Hugo van der Goes was a lay brother.

He was known to drink, which made things worse.
Says the same.

This is even a disquisition on the maladies of the life of art, if Writer says so.

Wanhope.

John Reed died of typhus.

Louise Bryant died of a cerebral hemorrhage.

Not even to a philosopher could old age be easy in the depths of poverty, Cicero said.
Nor could a fool find it anything but burdensome even amid ample wealth.

Maria Jeritza was the first Tosca to sing *Vissi d'arte* while lying on the floor.
Only because she had been elbowed off a couch by accident.

It was from God, Puccini decided.

Though with Jeritza also flaunting far too much obvious posterior, put in Geraldine Farrar.

Venus Callipyge.

Louise O'Murphy.

Tiepolo and Francesco Guardi were brothers-in-law.

Richard Wright died of a heart attack.

The question of Mikhail Sholokhov's authorship of *The Quiet Don*.
The question of Dmitri Shostakovich's authorship of his *Memoirs*.

St. Teresa of Lisieux knew *The Imitation of Christ* by heart.

John Masefield died of gangrene at eighty-eight when he refused to have an injured leg amputated.

Schopenhauer played the flute.

He has no insight into character. And no dramatic talent. His dialogue hardens to wood and stone.
Said Emerson about its author after reading *Oliver Twist*.

Camille Saint-Saëns talked with a lisp.

Mahler, discovering that Alma was having an affair with Walter Gropius.
And spending an entire day discussing it with Freud.

Is Macbeth impotent?

Hans Memling. That very model of a major minor master, as Erwin Panofsky had it.

The legend that as an impoverished, wounded soldier, Memling had begun to paint in gratitude to monks who sheltered him.

Edward Arlington Robinson died of pancreatic cancer.

Warren's Blacking.
30, Strand.

Carl Maria von Weber died of tuberculosis.

Ambrose Bierce fought at Shiloh, Stones River, and Chickamauga. And was wounded at Kenesaw Mountain.

The History of Rome Hanks and Kindred Matters.

Leonidas and the Three Hundred, who would perish at Thermopylae.
Only men who had already fathered sons to leave behind had been permitted to join the command.

Said of George Washington, at the height of the war with the British:
He sometimes throws and catches a ball for whole hours with his aides-de-camp.

Nabokov appears to have died of an infection caught in a hospital where he was being treated for the flu.

Paul Bowles died of a heart attack.

this is not

Jane Bowles died after a stroke.

Friday is on their island with Robinson Crusoe for thirteen out of Crusoe's twenty-eight years.

Why does Defoe not let him ever learn to speak more than pidgin English?

Why does Stephen Crane never actually state that the battle in *The Red Badge of Courage* is Chancellorsville?

La Scala was severely bombed in World War II.

The Vienna Staatsoper was severely bombed in World War II.

There are so few people who know how to make art. —Julian Schnabel.

One less than he thinks. —Robert Hughes.

In *Coriolanus,* Shakespeare allows someone to mention Cato.

Three centuries ahead of time.

> *And I will come out to meet you*
> *As far as Cho-fu-Sa.*

Pericles died of plague.

Stefan Lochner purchased a house in Cologne in 1442.

Konrad Witz purchased a house in Basel in 1443.

Martin Schongauer purchased a house in Colmar in 1477.

Hans Baldung Grien purchased a house in Strasbourg in 1527.

Paganini died of what was evidently cancer of the larynx.

Walter Pater died of gout.

It is written in a careless and humble style, in the vulgar tongue, which even housewives speak.
Said Dante of the *Comedy.*

William Etty.

The Axion Esti.

All through the night Rome went burning. Put that in the noontide and it loses some of its age-old significance, does it not?

Archaeological evidence for the historical reality of Gilgamesh.

Pergolesi died of consumption at twenty-six.

Laborare est Orare. Work is Worship.
Said the old monks.

Benedetto Croce died of a stroke.

this is not

Robert Schumann died mad, probably from syphilis.

Behold, this dreamer cometh.

Sophocles' father manufactured swords.

John Dos Passos died of congestive heart failure.

Tyndale was permitted the indulgence of being strangled at the stake before they set fire to him.

A Farewell to Arms:
1590, George Peele's version dating from.

Trying to imagine the shape of the modern world if Charles Martel had been defeated at Tours.

Simone Weil's final hospitalization was ostensibly for tuberculosis and exhaustion. Nevertheless a coroner's report labeled her death suicide by starvation.

The woman was mad, de Gaulle said.

Mantegna used a corpse as the model for one of his Crucifixions.
Géricault used several while painting *The Raft of the Medusa.*

Veit Stoss died blind. And destitute.

The almost unparalleled contemporary popularity of Euripides.

Greek soldiers captured and held as slaves after the disastrous expedition at Syracuse were actually given their freedom if they could teach passages from his plays from memory.

Which *many* could.

George Eliot translated Spinoza.
Emma Lazarus translated Judah Halevi.

Willem de Kooning's father was a beer distributor.

An incidental notation of Malcolm Lowry's, while describing a visit to a room used by De Quincey in the Lake District:

Smoking Prohibited.

> *She only said, My life is dreary,*
>   *He cometh not, she said;*
> *She said, I am aweary, aweary,*
>   *I would that I were dead.*

Cousin Ruddy was habitually foul-mouthed.

Flannery O'Connor died of lupus.

In the century after their deaths, Ben Jonson's name appeared in print three times as often as Shakespeare's.

Salathiel Pavy.

Why does Joyce let Leopold Bloom think Saverio Mercadante was Jewish?

April 26, 1937. A Monday.
Which was also Guernica's market day, drawing peasants in from the nearby countryside.

No matter how frequently, always given pause at remembering there is no color whatsoever in the canvas.

A little, plain, provincial, sickly-looking old maid.
Being Charlotte Brontë, as seen by George Henry Lewes.

Robert Southey died of—quote—softening of the brain.

And what should they know of England who only England know?

Gauguin once tried to kill himself with arsenic.
But vomited.

Do you think up that material when you're drunk?
Asked a cousin of Faulkner's.

Dittersdorf, you're not in tune.

Tintoretto died of what appears to have been stomach cancer.

Trollope died of a stroke.

Milledgeville, Georgia.

Tracts free as the Lord supplies the funds.

Frank Lloyd Wright died of a heart attack after surgery.

Hilda Doolittle died of the flu, though already assaulted by a heart attack and a stroke.

Even after *Einstein on the Beach* had been performed at the Metropolitan Opera, Philip Glass was driving a taxi in New York City.

Hypatia, who was battered to death by Christian fanatics.

Tantum religio potuit suadere malorum, Lucretius said. Such are the evils that religion prompts.

Emotion recollected in tranquility.

The best words in the best order.

Vivaldi died of no one knows what.
Of *internal fire*, the 1741 Vienna church registry having poetically settled for.

A social and moral pervert, Theodore Roosevelt called
Tolstoy.

Roosevelt on Henry James:
A miserable little snob.

On Thomas Paine:
A filthy little atheist.

Spinoza's tomb. At the Nieuwe Kerk in The Hague.

It was falling, too, upon every part of the lonely church-
yard on the hill where Michael Furey lay buried.

S. Y. Agnon died of a heart attack.

Dostoievsky's second wife, Anna, adding a note of
charm to a recollection of Dostoievsky pawning something:
　He sat there for over an hour—my poor, poor Fedya. So
sweet, and so brilliant and altogether fine, and he had to
sit and wait among a lot of Jews.

Stuck-groove music.

When the canvas is on the floor, I feel closer to it.
Said Jackson Pollock.

Marie Corelli was Charles Mackay's daughter.
Marcia Davenport was Alma Gluck's.

Robert Penn Warren died of prostate cancer.

Joshua Reynolds died blind.
After having been deaf through most of his life.

Only when the world itself is destroyed will the verses
of Lucretius perish.
Said Ovid.

Richard Brinsley Sheridan died profoundly in debt.
Yet was granted a spectacular Westminster Abbey
funeral.

Molière died after bursting a blood vessel in a convul-
sive tubercular coughing fit and choking on his own
blood.

Panta rei, ouden menei.

It is very difficult to understand and appreciate the generation that follows you, Matisse said.

I only know that summer sang in me
A little while, that in me sings no more.

The candle-end was flickering out in the battered can-
dlestick, dimly lighting up in the poverty-stricken room
the murderer and the harlot who had so strangely been
reading together in the eternal book.

this is not

The friendship of Byron and Stendhal.

According to Herodotus, Xerxes literally ordered that the Hellespont be given three hundred lashes when a storm washed away a bridge he had only then constructed for his invasion of the West.
And as an incidental afterthought also ordered his chief engineers beheaded.

Gary Cooper died of lung cancer.

Wilhelm Reich died in Lewisburg Penitentiary.

Mary Wollstonecraft Godwin died after giving birth to the infant girl who would one day marry Shelley.
Mary Wollstonecraft Godwin died after giving birth to the infant girl who would one day write *Frankenstein.*

Fanny Brawne's mother died in an accident in which her clothing caught on fire.

Things from which one would avert one's eyes even in a brothel.
Said Aretino in a letter to Michelangelo condemning *The Last Judgment.*

Which at least three different popes subsequently came close to having removed.

Rarely remembering that it was Congreve who said Music hath charms to soothe the savage breast.

Rarely remembering that it was Congreve who said
Hell hath no fury like a woman scorned.
In the same play.

People none of whose business it is repeatedly excising
the *Hughes* from the Yorkshire gravestone inscribed
Sylvia Plath Hughes.

Moses Mendelssohn died of a stroke.

Felix Mendelssohn died of a stroke.

Slabtown, Tennessee, Grace Moore was born in.

If on a winter's night with no other source of warmth
Writer were to burn a Roy Lichtenstein—qualms?

Qualmless.

Kierkegaard was regularly beaten up by his schoolmates.
Yeats *aussi.*

Christina Rossetti died while praying.

Se una notte d'inverno un viaggiatore.

The Muses' darling, Peele called Marlowe.

O Rare Ben Jonson.

this is not

So it befell in that affray that the said Ingram, in defence of his life, with the dagger aforesaid of the value of 12d. gave the said Christopher then & there a mortal wound over his right eye of the depth of two inches & of the width of one inch; of which mortal wound the aforesaid Christopher Morley then & there instantly died.

Negative capability.

Sartre died blind.
Having been strabismic.

Like Menander.

Splendid rooms and elegant furnishings are for people who have no thoughts, Goethe said.

Even in a palace it is possible to live well, said Marcus Aurelius.

If you've got no passport you're officially dead.

Ludwig Boltzmann took piano lessons from Anton Bruckner.

Eleanor Bull's.
Deptford Strand.

Andrew Marvell died of what was called tertian ague.
Probably meaning malaria.
Which his physician misdiagnosed.

Thackeray died of what was called a cerebral effusion.
Meaning either a brain hemorrhage or a stroke.

Jacob Barsimson. New Amsterdam, August 1654.

Lasse Viren.

No one, in any language, has ever written a novel that
equals or even approaches *Clarissa*, said Rousseau.
On a shelf with the Bible, Euripides, and Sophocles,
said Diderot of the same book.

Hannah Arendt died of a heart attack.

Watteau died of tuberculosis.

The little Marcel, at fourteen, asked to name life's
greatest unhappiness:
To be separated from *maman*.

Dear Sir:
I am sitting in the smallest room of my house. Your
review is before me. Shortly it will be behind me.

Did the American Indian not have the wheel?

Dies Irae.

A presumptuous mediocrity, Tchaikovsky called
Brahms.

Undoubtedly the best woman poet of our time, Hardy called Charlotte Mew.

How does Gertrude know all of the physical details of Ophelia's death with such exactness?

Soldiers! An innocent man is being degraded! Soldiers! An innocent is dishonored! Long live France!

Zola never met Dreyfus.

Max Reger.

Petrarch's copy of Virgil, with a marginal note in his own handwriting about the death of Laura in the Black Death, is still extant in a library in Milan.

The graves stood tenantless, and the sheeted dead
Did squeak and jibber in the Roman streets.

Or an ersatz prose alternative to *The Waste Land*, if Writer so suggests.

William of Ockham also died in the Black Death.

Robert Burns had nine illegitimate children.

Goya had nineteen *legitimate* children, by one wife. And several others otherwise.

Augustus John's habit of patting every passing London youngster on the head:

In case it is one of mine.

Brainsick. Troilus's word for Cassandra in *Troilus and Cressida.*

Lowell, Massachusetts, James McNeill Whistler was born in.

Lowell, Massachusetts, Jack Kerouac was born in.

Dies irae, dies illa
Solvet saeclum in favilla.

In one of his reincarnations, Pythagoras was a fish. And in another a bird.

He said.

Met him pike hoses.

In 1537, François Rabelais taught a course on Hippocrates at the school of medicine in Montpellier. In Greek.

Diego Rivera's affair with Paulette Goddard.

Diego Rivera's affair with Louise Nevelson.

Arrangement in Grey and Black No. 1: The Artist's Mother.

To be precise.

You ever read that, that *Cousin Bette*? Should I go on with it?

Virtually every inadequacy in recent French literature is due to absinthe, Daudet said in the late 1800s.

Annals I 65. Where Tacitus actually does, does, call a spade *an implement for digging earth and cutting turf.*

Paul Klee died of cardiac arrest after years of enduring scleroderma.

Sarah Orne Jewett died of a cerebral hemorrhage.

Thomas of Celano.

I have wasted all my youth chained to this tomb. Michelangelo protested to Julius II.

L'homme est né libre, et partout il est dans les fers.

Why hasn't Writer ever known? What is the black liquid that spills out of the dead Emma Bovary's mouth?

O death, where is thy sting at?

Les Rougon-Macquart.

Montesquieu died of pneumonia.

Eliot pursued graduate studies in the philosophy of F. H. Bradley, in part at Merton College, Oxford, where Bradley was still a lifetime fellow.

Presumably ignoring the rumor that Bradley went about at night shooting people's cats.

Wallace Stegner died after an automobile crash.

Bradley died of blood poisoning.

Liam O'Flaherty was shell-shocked on the Western Front in World War I.

Roger Bacon probably did not invent eyeglasses.

Forgetting, when starting to reread *The Hamlet*, that her name before the end will become Eula Varner Snopes.
And that in a later Snopes novel she will shoot herself.

Richard Bentley died of pleurisy.

The maniac who went at Rembrandt's *Night Watch* with a bread knife in the Rijksmuseum in 1975.
His counterpart who slashed a Barnett Newman in a different Amsterdam museum in 1986—and another Newman in the same museum a decade later.

No one ever put up a statue of a critic.
Said Sibelius.

this is not

Elderly, shabby, obscure, disreputable, pursued by debts, with only a noisy tenement room to work in.

Being a description by Gerald Brenan of the man who was writing *Don Quixote.*

The apparent evidence that two of Cervantes' sisters, and a niece, and his illegitimate daughter, became prostitutes—and in the very period of the book's first success.

Frida Kahlo's affair with Leon Trotsky.

The best French novelist of their era, Gide called Simenon.

Leaving moot the question of which of the man's more than five hundred novels he had in mind.

Stop pawing me, she said. You old headless horseman Ichabod Crane.

Rilke was devoted to polishing furniture.
Jackson Pollock baked pies.

Origen castrated himself.

No artist tolerates reality, Camus said.

Virgil spent seven years writing the *Georgics.*
Meaning an average of one line per day.

Pablo Neruda died of leukemia.

Nazim Hikmet died of a heart attack.

How beautiful yellow is!
Says a van Gogh letter.

Sortes Virgilianae.

Childe Roland to the Dark Tower Came.

Curfew Must Not Ring Tonight.

Dorothy L. Sayers died of a stroke.

If we regard the Fish as a Divine Life symbol of imme-morial antiquity, we shall not go very far astray.

Jack Johnson died in an automobile crash.

Nikos Kazantzakis died of the flu.

Jessie Laidlay Weston.

Laurence Sterne's realization roughly a third of the way through *Tristram Shandy* that the book lacks a preface. Whereupon he inserts one right where he is.

Jack Donne's transparently excessive eulogy for his patron's young daughter—whom he had never met or even seen.

If it had been written of ye Virgin Marie it had been something, Jonson told him.

William Saroyan died of prostate cancer.

Somerset Maugham once had four plays running simultaneously in London.

How much greater than it already is would the *Odyssey* seem if there had never happened to be an *Iliad* for it to be compared with?

St. John of the Cross was the son of a weaver.

J. Robert Oppenheimer died of throat cancer.

Maugham died of a stroke.

At last she grew common and infamous and gott the Pox, of which she died.
Says Aubrey's *Brief Lives* of one Elizabeth Broughton.

Paper will put up with anything that's written on it.
Said Stalin.

The best geometer in the world, Hobbes claimed Descartes could have become.
But that he had no head for philosophy.

Kurt Weill died of a heart attack.

Turner was considerably less than fastidious about cleanliness.

The Reader.
Being Aristotle's nickname at Plato's Academy.

A colt that kicks its mother.
Being what Plato personally called him after an early disagreement.

Samuel ha-Nagid.

Say it *out* for God's sake and have done with it.
Said William James to Henry.

Molokai. June 1885.
We lepers.

Anagnostes.

No Man is my name, and No Man they call me.

A Walk in the Sun.

A decade after Nelson's death at Trafalgar, Emma Hamilton died in poverty.

Archaeological evidence for the historical reality of Susan Sontag.

St. Catherine of Siena was illiterate.

Kafka was a vegetarian.

The English think soap is civilization.
Treitschke said.

Theodore Roethke died of a coronary occlusion.

At least one Boston newspaper suggested in all serious-
ness that Whitman should be horsewhipped for *Leaves of
Grass*.

Charlotte Salomon died in Auschwitz at twenty-six.

Pavel Friedman died in Auschwitz at nineteen. Or
younger.

Would Moe Berg really have shot Heisenberg?

Góngora died of apoplexy.

Balzac wrote more than two thousand characters into
his *Comédie humaine*.

There are 260,430 words in *Ulysses*.

Calvin died of hemorrhages of the lungs.

Oswiecim.

Exeunt.

Molière was never elected to the French Academy.
Balzac was never elected to the French Academy.

Was it John Searle who called Jacques Derrida the sort
of philosopher who gives bullshit a bad name?

I love the smell of napalm in the morning.

Josquin des Prez.

It took ten years after her suicide for Jeanne
Hébuterne's family to allow her remains to be reburied
beside Modigliani's in the Jewish section of Père Lachaise.

Adelaide Procter. Mrs. Henry Wood.

Géricault died after a fall from a horse.

Hindemith died of a stroke.

Nebuchadnezzar. Who razed Jerusalem.
And went mad.
And ate grass.

Cardinal Spellman of New York once sent Pope Pius
XII a Cadillac automobile with solid gold door handles.

Wyatt Earp died of chronic cystitis.

*Because night is here and the barbarians have
not appeared.*

Charles Lamb's insuperable proclivity to gin, Carlyle
termed it.

Frobisher. Hawkins. Drake.

Hitler typed with two fingers.
Mencken typed with two fingers.

Beethoven washed excessively.

Penthesilea.

The speculation that Dante spent time in Paris.
Or even at Oxford.

The possibility that on a political mission that took
him to Florence, Chaucer met Boccaccio.

Charlotte Corday was a great-grandniece of Corneille.
And devoted the morning to reading Plutarch at his
bloodiest before stabbing Marat.

Or a treatise on the nature of man, if Writer so labels it.

He had catched a great cold, had he no other clothes to
wear than the skin of a bear not yet killed.
Said Thomas Fuller.

Potatoes were not known in ancient Rome.
Tomatoes were not known in ancient Rome.
Oranges were not known in ancient Rome.

Hume died of what was probably colon cancer.

Edgar Degas never learned which side won World War I.
Piet Mondrian never learned which side won World
War II.

Flicka von Stade.

Manet died of tertiary syphilis.

Truman Capote died of heart disease complicated by
drug abuse.

Marianne Moore taught stenography at the Carlisle
Indian School, in Pennsylvania, when Jim Thorpe was a
student.
And fifty years later would remember that he held a
door for her.

Debussy's first wife shot herself.
As had a mistress, earlier.

Caedmon was illiterate.

The rue Descartes, Paul Verlaine died in.

Avenue Émile Zola, Paul Celan's last Paris address was on.

A *calle* in Madrid was renamed in honor of Vicente Aleixandre while he was still living there.

Herman Melville Boulevard is where, in Manhattan?

Twelve blocks north from the wishful-thinking intersection of Mark Rothko Road and Hart Crane Place.

The poetical fame of Ausonius condemns the taste of his age, Gibbon said.

But specially his wife lay sore upon him to attempt the thing, as she that was very ambitious, burning in unquenchable desire to bear the name of a Queen.

—Adding up to the sum total of what Shakespeare found in Holinshed from which he created Lady Macbeth.

The friendship of Paula Becker and Clara Westhoff.

Claudia Muzio was illegitimate.

Jenny Lind was illegitimate.

Voltaire's second wife was his own sister's daughter.

A passing thought of Kurt Vonnegut's, *re* Princess Diana:

Do we know if she ever read a book?

Title of an unfinished composition by Charles Ives:
Giants vs. Cubs, August 1907, Polo Grounds.

Ives died of heart disease compounded by diabetes.

Well, Bourrienne, you too will be immortal.
Why, General Bonaparte?
Are you not my secretary?
Tell me the name of Alexander's.
Hm, that is not bad, Bourrienne.

Haydn's father was a wheelwright.

The legend that Donatello almost supernaturally
refused to die until his commonplace crucifix could be
replaced by one carved by Brunelleschi.

But go, and if you listen she will call.

Eight people appeared at Robert Musil's funeral.

F. Scott Fitzgerald died of a sequence of heart attacks.
His most recent royalty statement showed seven copies
of *The Great Gatsby* sold during the preceding six
months.

The claim that John Wesley preached more than forty
thousand sermons.

this is not

Marc Blitzstein. Elliott Carter. Aaron Copland. David Diamond. Roy Harris. Walter Piston. Roger Sessions. Virgil Thomson.

All studied with Nadia Boulanger at Fontainebleau.

Dave Brubeck studied with Arnold Schoenberg and with Darius Milhaud.

Corbière died of tuberculosis at thirty.

Novalis died of tuberculosis at twenty-eight.

Laforgue was twenty-seven.

Basically every justification for persecution on the part of the Inquisition was at hand in St. Augustine.

As anyone's justification for censorship is ready in Plato.

J. R. R. Tolkien died of a chest infection while hospitalized for something else.

Ausonius once composed a poem to his writing paper.

The literary fame of *The Bonfire of the Vanities* condemns the taste of its age.

Mary Mapes Dodge.

Index Librorum Prohibitorum.

Don't come to us with your troubles. If you can't make enough money to live on, you can jump out the window or drown yourself.

Which Maria Callas vehemently denied having said to her mother.

The vasty hall of death.

Émile Verhaeren died in a fall under a train.

Arcangelo Corelli owned paintings by Bruegel and Poussin.

Adrienne Lecouvreur died of what was apparently rectal cancer.

Though in the Cilèa opera is poisoned, which had been a rumor.

But in either event was buried by torchlight in a field beside the Seine—as an actress, forbidden sanctified ground.

Maria Caniglia. Magda Olivero. Renata Tebaldi.

One of St. Teresa of Ávila's grandfathers was Jewish.

Jongkind died mad.

this is not

Hugo Wolf died mad.

Blake, at their only meeting, *re* Constable's pencil sketches: Why, this is not drawing, but inspiration.
I always meant it for drawing, Constable said.

The peculiar immortality of Sulpicia.
Six love poems, totaling only forty lines, and customarily tacked onto the collected work of Tibullus.
For two full thousand years.

Callas died in Paris, of a heart attack.
And was buried from a Greek Orthodox church on the rue Georges Bizet.

Tatiana Troyanos died of cervical cancer.

Writer's pleasure in realizing that the translation of Rabelais he most recently read was done by the father of Tanaquil LeClercq.

The Hay Wain.

Billie Holiday died of a kidney infection after years of heroin abuse.

Mornings, when the leaves are dewy, some of them are like jewels where the earliest sunlight glistens.

Who but my darling Greensleeves!

a   n o v e l   *117*

And Arthur was so bloody, that by his shield there might no man know him, for all was blood and brains on his sword.

Sir Thomas Urquhart. Peter Motteux.

Did Miss Linda Stillwagon ever see the poem?

John Singer Sargent died reading Voltaire.

Please, sir, I want some more.

Does Temple Drake ever go back and graduate from the University of Mississippi?

Merle Hapes. Junie Hovious.

Is it in *The Merry Wives of Windsor*, where *Greensleeves* is mentioned? Even twice?

Gluck died after a series of strokes.

Worms feed on Hector brave.

Siegfried Sassoon threw his Military Cross into the Mersey in disgust with the waste of war.

Mina Loy, already suffering advanced spinal osteoarthritis, died of pneumonia.

In one of his less balanced periods, Robert Lowell penciled in some revisions in Milton's *Lycidas*.

And insisted he was the author of the entire poem.

An anthology of extraordinary suicide notes.
Or of any suicide notes. Is there such?

Dorothy Parker died of a heart attack.

Kenneth Tynan died of emphysema.

He doesn't want me to have a life of my own.
Says Sonia Tolstoy's *Diary*.

Machiavelli died of unidentified stomach spasms.

Addie Joss died of tubercular meningitis.

Are we ever told what Addie Bundren dies of?

Lawrence Durrell was found dead in a bathroom.

Paulette Goddard died of heart failure.

Why does Writer sometimes seem to admire the *Iliad* even more when he is thinking about it than when he is actually reading it?

Augustus Montague Toplady.

Ignorant asses, John Webster repudiated the Eliza-
bethan theater audience as.

Get thee to a brewery.

Sailing the circumference of Lake Geneva, Byron and
Shelley took time to pay homage at the house in Lausanne
where Gibbon had written a great deal of *The Decline and
Fall.*

Hey, Dad, sharp this for me, please?

Theodore Watts-Dunton was said to sometimes hide
Swinburne's shoes—as a way of keeping him from
drinking.

From the King James Ecclesiastes:
One generation passeth away, and another generation
cometh: but the earth abideth for ever.
From the Revised Standard Version:
A generation goes and a generation comes, but the
earth remains forever.

From the King James Song of Solomon:
Our vines have tender grapes.
From the Revised Standard:
Our vineyards are in blossom.

James Baldwin died of cancer of the esophagus.

Michael Harrington died of cancer of the esophagus.

S. S. *Orizaba.*

You never have music here, do you.
It makes me nervous.

Mozart was addicted to billiards.

Frances Farmer died of throat cancer.

Martha Argerich.

André Breton died of heart failure precipitated by
massive asthma attacks.

Eddie Poe, Edgar Allan was commonly called.

Leslie Howard died in a plane shot down by the Germans in World War II.

William Gaddis died of prostate cancer.

Velázquez was unconditionally dismissive of Raphael
as a painter.

George Meredith died of what was called a chill.

Arrigo Boito died after catching the same in church.

John Gay died of what was called colic but was most probably stomach cancer.

Wallace Stevens once worked briefly as a newspaper reporter.
And was assigned to cover Stephen Crane's funeral.

Zane Grey was a dentist.

This skull is Helen.

Divinités du Styx.

Art which is not propaganda is not art, said Diego Rivera.

Writer's arse.

Edgairpo.

For a time as young men Delacroix and Bonington shared a studio.

Tony Lazzeri died in a fall down a flight of stairs during an epileptic seizure.

Early in the morning I go to the rear blackboard and draw a small dollar sign. No one notices. The janitor who washes the blackboards every night must surely guess why it's there.

Rachel Carson died of breast cancer.

St. Perpetua. Requesting a pin to fasten her hair—before guiding the gladiator's sword to her throat in the arena at Carthage.

Thomas More. Jesting on the scaffold and lifting aside his beard—before being beheaded.

Was Bede the first historian to date events B.C. and A.D.?

Lotte Lenya died of abdominal cancer.

Teresa Stratas had essentially camped out at her bedside for weeks, so that she would not die alone.

I shall not cease to fear Carthage until I know it is utterly destroyed, Cato said.

A son of Ring Lardner's died fighting with the Lincoln Brigade in Spain in 1938.

A son of Ring Lardner's died as a correspondent when his jeep hit a mine in World War II.

Sibelius died of a cerebral hemorrhage.

Pauline Viardot. Who sang the first performance of Brahms' *Alto Rhapsody*.

And may have had an illegitimate child by Turgenev.

Johann Uhr, the Royal Armorer.

Ford Madox Ford died of heart failure.

The Cartesian Soul of Frank Sinatra.
Having been the subtitle of an actual academic paper delivered at Hofstra University in 1998.

Dear God! the very houses seemed asleep.

A daughter of Theodor Herzl's died in Theresienstadt.

A daughter of Theodor Herzl's.

One of Edvard Munch's sisters went mad.

Hogarth died of a ruptured artery.

I owe the discovery that I was a Jew more to Gentiles than Jews, Einstein said.

A public meeting was held in Florence in 1504 to decide on the placement of Michelangelo's *David.* Detailed minutes still exist showing that Leonardo, Piero di Cosimo, Filippino Lippi, Sansovino, Botticelli, Lorenzo di Credi, and Perugino all had something to say.
The decision was finally left to Michelangelo.

A blessed thing.
Said Elizabeth Barrett Browning, of opium.

Half in love with easeful Death.

Vaslav Nijinsky died of kidney failure after decades of insanity.

O. Henry died penniless.

The North Sea, Karl Marx's ashes were scattered in.

Djuna Barnes Drive. Anne Sexton Street.

Calcutta, Thackeray was born in.
Bombay, Kipling was.

Gaspara Stampa died of what may have been cancer of the womb.

Ovid left twice as much work as any other Roman poet.
And said he had destroyed endless pages more, as unsatisfactory.

Henry Purcell died of consumption.

Francis Thompson died of consumption.

Richard Savage died in debtors' prison.

The volume of Sophocles from Shelley's pocket when he was drowned is in the Bodleian Library at Oxford.
The Keats was burned with his corpse at Viareggio.

The Keats had been borrowed from Leigh Hunt.

Alejo Carpentier died of throat cancer.

Kant was never in his life in the vicinity of a mountain. It appears probable that he never saw the ocean either.

Venus clerk, Ovyde,
That hath ysowen wonder wyde
The grete god of Loves name.

Marilyn Horne's tale that the first time she was asked to sing *Semiramide* the only way she could get her hands on a score was to steal it from the Los Angeles Public Library.

In the four quarters of the globe, who reads an American book?
Asked Sydney Smith in 1819.

Melville's father died mad.

Schopenhauer's father jumped out of a window.

The long martyrdom of being trampled to death by geese, Kierkegaard called reading one's reviews.

Berchtesgaden.

Juden raus!

The God that holds you over the pit of Hell, much as
one holds a spider, or some loathsome insect over the fire,
abhors you, and is dreadfully provoked.

Milo of Crotona.

The greatest painter of our era, Magritte called Giorgio
de Chirico.
Unsurprisingly.

Jacob Epstein died of heart failure.

Carl Gustav Jung died of heart failure.

Every morning the author of *Faust* and *Werther* kisses
me. In the afternoon I play for him for about two hours.
Noted Felix Mendelssohn, at twelve.

> *Hold off! unhand me, grey-beard loon!*
> *Eftsoons his hand dropt he.*

Derek Lindsay was who?

Longfellow died of peritonitis.

Frank Norris died of peritonitis.

Selma Lagerlöf died of peritonitis.

Es inevitable la muerta del Papa.

Béla Bartók died of leukemia.

Charles Péguy was killed leading a charge in the first battle of the Marne.

Alexander, young, broke Bucephalus—whom no one else could sit—simply by perceiving that he balked at his own shadow and riding him into the sun.

Nonlinear. Discontinuous. Collage-like. An assemblage.
Self-evident enough to scarcely need Writer's say-so.

Obstinately cross-referential and of cryptic interconnective syntax.
Here perhaps less than self-evident to the less than attentive.

Ulrich Friedrich Richard von Wilamowitz-Moellendorf.

Laurence Sterne died of pleurisy, after years of lung hemorrhages.

Rousseau died of a stroke.

The Private Papers of Henry Ryecroft.

Gilles de Rais. Who was a marshal of France at twenty-five.

this is not

And fought by Joan's side at Orleans.
And.

Baudelaire often wore pink gloves.

Martha Constantine, a handsome young woman, was treated with great indecency and cruelty by several of the troops, who first ravished, and then killed her by cutting off her breasts. These they fried, and set before some of their comrades, who ate them without knowing what they were.
Records *Fox's Book of Martyrs*.

Clausewitz died of cholera.

The Prince, the King, the Emperor, the God Almighty of novelists.
Wilkie Collins called Walter Scott.

Robin Vote.

Vom Kriege.

Walter Benjamin and Gertrud Kolmar were cousins.

Monet dropped from the skies on me with a collection of magnificent pictures. I am now lodging two impecunious artists, for Renoir is also here. It's like a nursing home. I love it.
Said a letter of Frédéric Bazille's—four years before he was killed at twenty-nine in the Franco-Prussian War.

Joe Tinker died of diabetes.

Johnny Evers died of a cerebral hemorrhage.

Frank Chance died of tuberculosis.

The population of Athens at the height of its accomplishments was at best two hundred and seventy-five thousand.
The population of Dante's Florence was probably forty thousand.

Abbotsford.

Piero della Francesca's *St. Agatha.* Tiepolo's. Zurbarán's.
Ambrogio Lorenzetti's.

Mary McCarthy died of lung cancer.

Hermann Prey died of a heart attack.

A double play gives you two twenty-sevenths of a ball game.
Pointed out Casey Stengel.

Harold Bloom's claim to the *New York Times* that he could read at a rate of five hundred pages per hour.

Writer's arse.

Spectacular exhibition! Right this way, ladies and gentlemen! See Professor Bloom read the 1961 corrected and reset Random House edition of James Joyce's *Ulysses* in one hour and thirty-three minutes. Not one page stinted. Unforgettable!

Parisian brothels. The only place where one's shoes were ever properly shined.
Said Toulouse-Lautrec.

Dryden, to a publisher:
I find all your trade are sharpers.

Was Plutarch the first writer ever to counsel kindness to animals?

The William Wordsworth Funeral Home, in Hollywood, F. Scott Fitzgerald was buried from.

Leonardo played the lyre.
So astonishingly well that his patron the Duke of Milan initially admired him more for that than for his art.

Modigliani and Soutine were once living in such penury that they shared a single cot.
Sleeping in shifts.

A second-rate mind, T. E. Lawrence ranked Shakespeare's as.

What's this? Can't spare an hour and a half? Wait, wait. Our matinee special, today only! Watch Professor Bloom eviscerate the Pears-McGuinness translation of Wittgenstein's *Tractatus*—eight minutes and twenty-nine seconds flat! Guaranteed.

Mine eyes have seen the glory
Of Rabindranath Tagore.

Paul Celan's visit to Todtnauberg.

Galileo died blind.

Journalist: May I see Georgia O'Keeffe?
Georgia O'Keeffe: You have.

Samuel Johnson, on criticism:
A fly, Sir, may sting a stately horse and make him wince, but one is but an insect, and the other is a horse still.

Gentes and laitymen, fullstoppers and semicolonials, hybreds and lubberds!

Louis Sockalexis was an epileptic.

Alfred Stieglitz died of a stroke.

The Samuel Butler who wrote *Hudibras* died in poverty.

A Latin translation of Marco Polo once belonging to Christopher Columbus is extant in Seville. With seventy marginal notes in Columbus's handwriting.
Mainly in regard to the whereabouts of treasure.

Jim Thorpe died of a heart attack.

Allowed out of his steel military cage at Pisa for exercise, Ezra Pound sometimes swung a broom handle as if it were a baseball bat.

Who do you make believe is pitching to you, Uncle Ez?
Can't you see Dizzy Dean out there, soldier?

From Suetonius, a description of Vespasian:
Habitually wearing the expression of someone who is straining at stool.

Meyer Lansky was a subscriber to the Book-of-the-Month Club.

Photography is not an art.

Writer talking to himself again.

As did Hölderlin, in addition to Yeats.

Writer suspects Hesoid likewise, even if long beyond any possibility of verification.

I bring you back Cathay!

Edwin Hubble died of a stroke.

Sir Alexander Fleming died of a heart attack.

The editor of *Novy Mir* began to read a prepublication copy of *One Day in the Life of Ivan Denisovich* in bed.
And then found himself so impressed that he not only got up but put on a suit and a necktie to finish with what he felt to be the requisite respect.

The Samuel Butler who wrote *Erewhon* died of pernicious anemia.

There seems to me too much misery in the world, said Darwin.

Cortés. 1519–1526:
Three hundred and fifteen soldiers. Sixteen horses. Seven cannon.

Of all books extant in all kinds, Homer is the first and best, Chapman said.

The sovereign poet, Dante called him.
Without being able to read Greek.

That fiery splendour of narrative which seems almost
to have died out of the world when the *Iliad* was complete, Gilbert Murray talked of.

Irving Berlin's father was a cantor.
Al Jolson's father was a cantor.

Berlin died at one hundred. Of age alone, evidently.

George Santayana died of stomach cancer.
Having spent his last years attended by Irish nuns at a
convent in Rome.

Will scholars of relatively recent English literature
have any idea three or four centuries from now how differ-
ently the names Yeats and Keats were pronounced?

Suzanne Valadon's affair with Puvis de Chavannes.
He fifty-seven. Valadon seventeen.

One of Wordsworth's brothers died in a shipwreck.
Another became master of Trinity College, Cambridge.

A brother of Walt Whitman's died mad.
Another was a lifelong imbecile.

Fragonard died of a cerebral hemorrhage.

Chardin died of dropsy.

Cavendish, Vermont.

A pansy with hair on his chest, Zelda Fitzgerald called Hemingway.
Ninety percent Rotarian, supplied Gertrude Stein.

George Bernard Shaw died at ninety-four of complications after breaking a hip.

Valadon died of a stroke.

Brian Moore died of pulmonary fibrosis.

Papal censors in 1817 refused to allow the heroine in Rossini's Cinderella opera to show her bare foot. The libretto had to be rewritten without the glass slippers.

Conchita Supervia. Teresa Berganza. Cecilia Bartoli.

Rarely remembering that it was Menander who said Whom the gods love die young.

Charles Brockden Brown sent Thomas Jefferson an inscribed copy of *Wieland*.

Telemann was Carl Philipp Emanuel Bach's godfather.

It is noteworthy that on the whole children love their parents less than their parents love them.
Perceived Hegel.

this is not

Richard Burton died of a cerebral hemorrhage.

Death-of-the-Month-Club.

Ensor died at eighty-nine.
Having done every bit of his significant work before he was forty.

Thomas Wolfe died of tuberculosis which had spread to the brain.

Clutching the stern of one of the withdrawing Persian galleys at Marathon, a brother of Aeschylus was killed when his hand was chopped off by an ax.

Giacomo Leopardi died of cholera.

C. Wright Mills died of a heart attack.

Tim the ostler.

St. Augustine's admission that even he could not comprehend God's purpose in creating flies.

Jan van Eyck died in Bruges in 1441.

Petrus Christus died in Bruges in 1472 or 1473.

Hans Memling died in Bruges in 1494.

Gerard David died in Bruges in 1523.

Through the dim purple air of Dante fly those who have stained the world with the beauty of their sin.
Said Oscar Wilde.

Dante is not worth the pains necessary to understand him.
Said Chesterfield.

Wilde died of encephalitic meningitis, almost certainly connected with syphilis.

Meg Merrilies.

Ceci n'est pas un conte. Diderot, 1772.
Ceci n'est pas une pipe. Magritte, 1929.

Wilbur Wright died of typhoid fever.

Orville Wright died of a heart attack.
Thirty-six years later.

Melville's spelling:
Don Quixotte.

August Strindberg was illegitimate.

Ulysses:
An illiterate, underbred book it seems to me, the book of a self-taught working man, and we all know how depressing they are.

Yes, Virginia.

Port Arthur, Texas, Robert Rauschenberg was born in.

Thelonious Monk died of a stroke.

Charles Mingus died of amyotrophic lateral sclerosis.

The *Oresteia.* Aeschylus was sixty-seven.
Orestes. The *Bacchae.* Euripides was seventy-six and seventy-seven.
Philoctetes. Oedipus at Colonus. Sophocles was well past eighty.

Hillerich and Bradsby.

Gandhi suffered from chronic constipation.
Henry James suffered from chronic constipation.
Freud suffered from chronic constipation.

Vixere fortes ante Agamemnona, Horace said.
There were brave men living before Agamemnon.

Aretino died of apoplexy.

Ariosto died of tuberculosis.

Le Douanier Rousseau once informed Picasso that they
two were the two greatest living painters:
I in the modern style and you in the Egyptian.

Nine in the third place indicates:
   The ridge beam sags to the breaking point.
   Adversity.

Renoir suffered from extreme rheumatism and threat-
eningly congested lungs, but died of a heart attack.

Gaetano Donizetti died mad.

Branwell—Emily—Anne—are gone like dreams—gone
as Maria and Elizabeth went twenty years ago. One by
one I have watched them fall asleep on my arm.
   Said Charlotte, late along.

   God is necessary and so must exist.
   Well, that's all right, then.
   But I know He doesn't and can't.
   That's more likely.

Epis.

Eleven of Ernest Rutherford's students became winners
of the Nobel Prize.

Hermann Hesse died in his sleep at eighty-five.

Catullus died at thirty.

Pascal wrote certain of the *Provincial Letters* twelve times.
Tolstoy did nine versions of his *Kreutzer Sonata.*

Le Douanier played the violin.

Patrick White died of bronchial collapse resulting from pleurisy.

Manet and Mallarmé spent time together virtually every afternoon for twenty years.

Sir Arthur Conan Doyle was evidently the first person in England ever to receive a ticket for speeding.

Das Glasperlenspiel.

Wittgenstein, it is you who are creating all the confusion!

Suzette Gontard died of tuberculosis.

Thoreau:
How many a man has dated a new era in his life from the reading of a book?

Marie Bashkirtseff died of consumption at twenty-four.

August Macke was killed in France in the first weeks of World War I.

Keith Douglas was killed by a mortar fragmentation bomb three days after the start of the Normandy Invasion.

Catalogue raisonné.

The scene in Hades in *Odyssey* XI where Odysseus tells Achilles of the extraordinary nervousness inside the Trojan Horse.
Except for Achilles' own son Neoptolemus, who cannot wait to attack.

The assumption, even in much of antiquity itself, that the mythic Horse had actually been some sort of engineer's device to breach the walls.

Arturo Toscanini died of a stroke.

Guido Cantelli died in an air crash.

Needing a few seconds to remember that it will be that same Neoptolemus who flings Hector's infant son from the battlements after the Greek victory.

Anaïs Nin died of cardiorespiratory arrest while enduring metastatic vaginal cancer.

Robert Frost died of a pulmonary embolism while enduring metastatic prostate cancer.

What interests me is the *anguish* of van Gogh, Picasso said.

Sir James Frazer died blind.

Thoreau died of tuberculosis.

Turner left a serious fortune to a fund for indigent artists. Relatives fought the will and won the money for themselves.

Why does Writer sometimes seem to admire *Ulysses* even more when he is thinking about it than when he is actually reading it?

A grace to say before reading Elie Wiesel's *Night*? Before Celan's *Todesfuge*?

Swinburne died of pneumonia.

Joseph Heller died of a heart attack.

Puccini and Mascagni were once roommates.
Mascagni would become a supporter of Mussolini. And finish his life in disgrace in a seedy Rome hotel.

Robert Burns was said to have died of alcoholism and/or venereal disease.

A hundred years later the symptoms were reread as those of heart disease stemming from childhood rheumatic fever.

Jean Armour.

John Bunyan died of an undiagnosed fever after being caught on horseback in a storm.

Kepler died of an undiagnosed fever after a considerable journey on horseback to collect money he was owed.

Whistler died of a heart condition.

Jack Kerouac died of a gastrointestinal hemorrhage from cirrhosis of the liver.

> *The grave's a fine and private place,*
> *But none, I think, do there embrace.*

Astyanax.

As a Marine pilot in Korea, Ted Williams several times flew as Colonel John Glenn's wing man.

Sophocles played ball with great skill, it says in Athenaeus.

He alters and retouches the same phrases incessantly, and paces up and down like a madman.
Reported a pupil of Chopin's.

Stanislaus Joyce died of a heart condition at seventy. On Bloomsday.

James Thurber died of a brain tumor.

Beau Brummell died mad.

Antoine Roquentin.

Thomas Hobbes did translations of Homer into English in his late eighties.
Not particularly well.

Eight Miles of Books.

Aristotle, asked what grows old most swiftly: Gratitude.

The Boudreau Shift.

Hobbes played the bass viol.

Ignazio Silone's parents died in an earthquake.

James Laughlin once changed a flat tire for Gertrude Stein.

Samuel Beckett once sat through a New York vs. Houston doubleheader at Shea Stadium.

I could die to-day, if I wished, merely by making a little effort, if I could wish, if I could make an effort.

Blake's insistence that at the age of four he had seen God watching him through a window.

Amy Lowell died of a stroke.

Vesalius was condemned to death by the Inquisition for dissecting humans. But was permitted to make a pilgrimage to the Holy Land in penance instead.
And then died en route home of overexposure after a shipwreck.

Sestos. Abydos.

St. Francis of Assisi probably died of malaria.

How vain it is, and how futile, to lament the dead.
Said Stesichorus.

William Burroughs killed his wife while trying to shoot a glass perched on her head à la William Tell.

The Egyptian *Book of the Dead.* From papyri and pyramid inscriptions dated as early as 1580 B.C.

Or a contemporary variant on the latter, if Writer says so.

Writer incidentally doing his best here—insofar as his memory allows—not to repeat things he has included in his earlier work.

Meaning in this instance the four hundred and fifty or more deaths that were mentioned in his last book also.

Burroughs died of heart failure.

Grover's Corners, New Hampshire.

Your last novel was a flop.

All of this preoccupation implying little more, presumably, than that Writer is turning older.

Stockholm, Greta Garbo's ashes were buried near.

They're going to cut a street through.
They would, Bill said.

Plutarch says that to force himself to study oratory, Demosthenes once shaved half his head—so that he would be too embarrassed to leave his house.

Though with Writer also now recalling the refrain from Dunbar's *Lament for the Makers*, about the deaths of such as Chaucer and Lydgate and Henryson and Gower:

Timor mortis conturbat me.
The fear of death distresses me.

And what is the use of a book, thought Alice, without pictures or conversations?

There is no such thing as a great movie. A Rembrandt is great. Mozart chamber music.
Said Marlon Brando.

Eliot died of emphysema in conjunction with a damaged heart.

Pound died of a blocked intestine.

Being less than surprised that Rouault began his career working at stained-glass windows.

She said he was a village explainer, excellent if you were a village, but if you were not, not.

Otello. Verdi was seventy-four.
Falstaff. Verdi was eighty.

Office of the Dead.

The friendship of John Donne and Isaak Walton.

Rudolph Valentino died of a perforated ulcer.

this is not

Trollope, as remembered by a schoolmate at Harrow:
Without exception the most slovenly and dirty boy I ever met.

Ben Shahn died of a heart attack after surgery.

Andy Warhol died after gallbladder surgery.

East Coker, for Eliot's ashes.

Roman Jakobson, in opposition to a novelist, namely Nabokov, teaching literature at Harvard:
Should an elephant teach zoology?

Arnold Schoenberg and George Gershwin were tennis partners.

John Donne. Anne Donne. Undone.

Camoëns died unknown and penniless in a plague.

A lieutenant of Alexander's, before the Battle of Arbela:
Don't think we fear their vast numbers, Sire. They'll not stand the stink of goat that clings to us.

For centuries, in England:
The burial of a suicide under a high road, ideally at a crossroads.
And with a wooden stake driven into his/her heart.

Bertolt Brecht wrote a poem about one of the Dempsey-Tunney fights.

Xanthippe was a shrew.
Living with her teaches me to get along with the rest of the world, Socrates said.

Gershwin died of a brain tumor.

Edward MacDowell died mad, probably from syphilis.

Manolete. Islero. Linares.

The wife of Johann Strauss, Jr., once asked Brahms for an autograph. Brahms sketched out the opening notations for the *Blue Danube.*
And signed them Alas, not by Johannes Brahms.

Ronsard me célébrait du temps que j'étais belle.

Wolfgang Pauli: You probably think these ideas are crazy.
Niels Bohr: Unfortunately they are not crazy enough.

Katyn.

Nanking.

Kyd's scene in *The Spanish Tragedy* where Hieronimo finds the corpse of his son hanged from a tree in his garden.

Luciano Pavarotti's inability to read music.

Ronsard died of gout.

Conan Doyle died of a heart condition.

Fichte once badly needed to borrow money from Kant. Kant said no.

Frederick Exley died of a stroke.

Joanna Baillie.

Auden was known to show up at the opera in a stained tuxedo and bedroom slippers.

Samuel Johnson died of dropsy.

Gregor Mendel died of dropsy.

Albert Pinkham Ryder lived in such filth, with even his bed spilling over with rubbish, that he generally slept on a patch of rug on the floor.

Willie Maugham, he was commonly called.

Archie MacLeish.

Joe DiMaggio died on Al Gionfriddo's birthday.

Scriabin died of a blood infection.

W. N. P. Barbellion.

Daydreaming of a MacArthur Foundation award.

Writer talking to himself yet another time.

As did Gogol, in addition to Yeats and Hölderlin and Hesiod.

Talkative, outgoing, inquisitive, formidably erudite, and sharp.

Stamford, Connecticut, Ezio Pinza died in.

Lakeville, Connecticut, Wanda Landowska died in.

That blockhead John Stuart Mill, Nietzsche anointed him.

Passage to India. 1871.
A Passage to India. 1924.

Then again Kant did help Fichte find a teaching post.

Jonas Salk died of heart failure.

O tu, Palermo.

George Gissing's father was a druggist.

I am a lost man! I whispered to myself. Ladies and gentlemen, I am a lost man! And I repeated that over and over as I went on jumping on my hat.

Augusta Leigh died in poverty.

Ouida died in poverty.

Mary Webb died in poverty.

Jane Avril died in poverty.

Jane Avril.

Monk Lewis died of yellow fever on board a ship in the Atlantic.

Two of the Le Nains died within two days of each other. The third would continue painting for twenty-nine more years.

Mill died of what was termed a local fever.

Hubert van Eyck died in 1426.
If there was a Hubert van Eyck.

Thorstein Veblen was once fired by the University of Chicago for—quote—womanizing.

Anaxagoras, in exile, when told that the Athenians had condemned him to death for impiety:
Nature long ago condemned them and me both.

Dashiell Hammett died of lung cancer.

Raymond Chandler died of pneumonia, hardly warded off by uncompromising alcoholism.

The Loss of the Eurydice.
Where Hopkins rhymes *portholes* and *mortals.*

Beckett died of complications from emphysema.

Einstein once gave private lectures to small groups in Prague.
Some of which included Kafka.

Montaigne could not swim.
Unfortunately neither could Shelley.

Dish-washings, Carlyle called Jane Austen's novels.
Swill, Steve Crane called Tennyson.

Antoine. Louis. Mathieu.

Orfamay Quest.

Sir Thomas Malory may have died in prison.

this is not

Vincenzo Bellini died of tuberculosis.
Or of an intestinal inflammation.

Handel owned a number of Rembrandts.

Schoenberg taught at the University of California at Los Angeles for eight years after leaving Nazi Germany.
And then was made to retire on a pension of $38 per month.

Rome has spoken. The debate is concluded.

How shall this be, seeing I know not a man?

The suspicion that Ambrose Bierce was a suicide. And perhaps did not even go to Mexico.

Teresa Guiccioli had hemorrhoids.

Edith Wharton and her husband used separate bedrooms.

Jones Very spent time in the same Boston insane asylum where Robert Lowell would be a patient a century later.

Doak Walker died after being paralyzed in a skiing accident.

Abba Kovner.

Rimsky-Korsakov died of a heart attack.

Leonard Bernstein died of a heart attack though already doomed by lung cancer.

A kind of shopgirl's philosophy, Lévi-Strauss dismissed much of Sartre as.
An ecstatic schoolgirl anti-style, Leslie Fiedler accused Kerouac of.

Wharton died of a series of strokes.

Burn down their synagogues. Banish them altogether. Pelt them with sow dung. I would rather be a pig than a Jewish Messiah.
Amiably pronounced Luther.

I told you not go with drunken goy ever.
Says the ghost of Leopold Bloom's father.

What the world would know of the Holocaust if the Germans had won.

Santa Maria delle Grazie, Milan. 1495–1498.

The fellow that was pilloried, I have forgot his name.

You can actually draw so beautifully. Why do you spend your time making all these queer things?
Picasso: That's why.

Give me a laundry list and I will set it to music.
Said Rossini.

The Girls in Their Summer Dresses.

The friendship of Menander and Epicurus.

St. Anthony was illiterate.
And did not bathe. Ever.

The exact route by which Hannibal crossed the Alps.
Which to this day historians have not determined.

Voltaire said he would believe in doctors when he met
one who was a centenarian.
Dying himself at eighty-four, of uremia.

A hundred devils trample me down if old drunkards do
not outnumber old doctors, Rabelais said.

Is Frans Hals the most documented drinker among
earlier artists?
Is Addison close to it among writers?

Walker Percy died of prostate cancer.

Lillian Nordica. The first American to sing at Bayreuth.
George London. The first American to sing *Boris
Godunov* at the Bolshoi.

Katherine Mansfield died of tuberculosis.

Rube Waddell died of tuberculosis.

July 14, 1789. There were seven prisoners, total, in the fortress.

A man can die but once; we owe God a death.

The Colossus of Rhodes crashed down in an earthquake in 224 B.C. Fully three centuries later Pliny the Elder would comment on the monstrous bronze fragments that still lay about the harbor.

George Herbert played the lute.

Nordica died of pneumonia after a shipwreck in the Malay Archipelago.

London died after years of paralysis from a stroke.

An intriguing speculation of La Fontaine's:
Was St. Augustine as wise as Rabelais?

Then Werther blew his silly brains out—unquote— while Charlotte went on cutting bread and butter.

Chares of Lindus.

Ann Rutledge died of typhoid fever. At nineteen.

Auden died of a heart attack in a hotel room.

Richard Tucker died of a heart attack in a hotel room.

Dirty, dull, and false.
Said R. L. S. of *Tom Jones*.

Yeats and Pound married cousins.
Coleridge and Southey married sisters.

Domenico Scarlatti died penniless. Farinelli saw to it
that his family was cared for.

Our American Cousin.

Stevie Smith died of a brain tumor.

Ava Gardner died of pneumonia.

1893. Sixty feet six inches.

Lillian Russell went out of her way to arrange to meet
Amos Rusie.

The anti-Semitic clause in the Magna Carta.

And mighty poets in their misery dead.

Dreiser died of a heart attack.

Mencken died of a heart attack.

Barbaric degrees of drinking, Arrian says Alexander took to by the end.

Edward Hopper Highway. Susanne Langer Mews.

Even Homer sometimes nods, Horace said.
Wordsworth sometimes wakes, Byron allowed.

Wordsworth on Byron in turn:
Perverted.

E. M. Forster died of a massive stroke.

Solomon Grundy.

I suppose my main source of annoyance with him was his affectation of not being a writer, but a farmer; this would have been pretentious even had he been a farmer.
Said Allen Tate, *re* Faulkner.

Correggio died either of heat prostration or from drink-ing foul water to relieve it.

Correggiosity.

The most stirring battle-poem in English is about a brigade of cavalry which charged in the wrong direction.
Said Orwell.

this is not

So certain was Pliny the Younger that the histories of Tacitus would last through the centuries that he pleaded with Tacitus to be mentioned in them.

The centuries presently numbering nineteen.

Runnymede.

Rydal Mount.

Jean-Baptiste Greuze died impoverished and forgotten.

Dawn Powell was buried in a potter's field.

Writer had but a glimpse of Faulkner.
As it happens, of Hemingway *también*.

I see no point in reading, said Louis XIV.

Pliny the Younger having been a nephew, not a son.

Ty Cobb died of prostate cancer.

Faulkner, at a funeral. Small and beady-eyed.
Hemingway at ringside.

Was Shane his first name or his last?

Faulkner in fact looking like a Eula Varner in-law.

Sit not down on the bushel.

You are leaving the American Sector.

Miguel de Unamuno died of a stroke.

Glenn Gould died of a stroke.

When and where did the last person die who still believed in the existence of Zeus?

Time flies like an arrow.
Fruit flies like a cantaloupe.

Green-wood Cemetery, in Brooklyn, Lola Montez is buried in.

Bronislaw Malinowski died of a heart attack.

Vittorio Gassman died of a heart attack.

Lincoln never saw Europe.

The one person in the world he would have liked to meet, Lenin said, was Charlie Chaplin.
The one person in the world he would have liked to meet, Eliot said, was Joe Louis.

Camille Pissarro died of blood poisoning.

Le Douanier died of blood poisoning after neglecting a cut.

Is there a single Jane Austen volume that manages not to bring up the subject of money before the end of page one?

The Odessa steps.

Isak Dinesen died of what was recorded as emaciation.

W. S. Gilbert died while trying to rescue someone from drowning.

How old was the Virgin Mary?

Rogier van der Weyden's panel of St. Luke sketching her portrait.

Clay Allison died of a broken neck.

Was Glenn Gould someone else who talked to himself, or would he have only been singing along?

Kenneth Rexroth's incomparably godawful verses on the premise that people who shopped at Brooks Brothers caused the death of Dylan Thomas.

Malcolm Lowry, on the same death:
We drank his health, poured a libation of gin to his memory, and for some reason cut down a tree, likewise dead, and an old friend.

Died on Saturday,
Buried on Sunday.

Rexroth died of a heart attack.

Jean Cocteau died of a heart attack.

The Brahms *German Requiem:*
Listening to it is a sacrifice that should be asked of a
man only once in his life, Shaw said.

Overheard, frequently, by Xenophanes:
How old were you when the Persians came?

Writer has actually written some relatively traditional
novels. Why is he spending his time doing this sort of
thing?
That's why.

But where is your friend, Daddy?

Melville's lifetime earnings from his fiction—from
more than forty-five years—would appear to barely exceed
ten thousand dollars.

Minnie Hauk died blind. And living on charity.

Lenin died of a cerebral hemorrhage.

Juvenal's poetry is not mentioned anywhere, by anyone, during his lifetime or until almost two hundred years after his death.

By the era of Petrarch and Boccaccio and Chaucer, he has become O Master Juvenal.

Words, words, words.

Vous sortez du Secteur Americain.

Does Lunita Laredo desert Major Brian Tweedy, or does she die young?

What time was it forty-five minutes before the beginning of time?

Wanamaker's department store, in Manhattan, Richard Strauss once conducted concerts in.

At Actium, what with the torching of a number of his ships, many of Antony's troops were roasted alive in their own red-hot armor, says Dio Cassius.

What a coarse, immoral, mean, and senseless work *Hamlet* is, Tolstoy said.

> *By brooks too broad for leaping*
> *The lightfoot boys are laid . . .*

Is *Clarissa* still the longest single novel in the language?

I must dye one day, and as good this day as another.
Says a suicide in Rowley.

Trade is wholly inconsistent with a gentleman's calling.
Said John Locke.

Salamis, Solon's ashes were scattered at.

Kipling died of a hemorrhage from duodenal ulcers.

Alfred de Musset died of heart failure.

Lope de Vega wrote what may have been as many as fifteen hundred plays. Of which almost a third survive.

Thomas Eakins made Walt Whitman's death mask.

Camerado is in no one's dictionary.

> *The rose-lipt girls are sleeping*
> *In fields where roses fade.*

Edmund Wilson died of a coronary occlusion.

Sir Thomas Beecham died of a stroke.

Silas Tomkyn Comberbache.
Being a fictitious name once used by Coleridge in the dragoons.

Kilgore Rosewater.
Being one used by Kurt Vonnegut in a hospital.

Bix Beiderbecke died of pneumonia while also con-
fronting delirium tremens.

Fichte died of an unspecified fever.

The friendship of René Char and Martin Heidegger.

Charlemagne could read but could not write.

Joan of Arc could do neither.

How old were you, what were you doing, when you
heard Lord Byron was dead?

Geneviève de Galard-Terraube.

Oliver Goldsmith played the flute.

Hopp, hopp! Hopp, hopp! Hopp, hopp!

The *Pervigilium Veneris.*

Gertrude Stein, to Jacques Lipchitz:
Besides Shakespeare and me, who do you think there is?

Luis Buñuel died of cancer of the bile duct and the liver.

Tennyson, at fifteen, etched it with a sharp stone into
the face of a boulder in the woods:
Byron is dead.

Samuel Pepys once smacked his wife in the eye.
In point of fact, on December 19, 1664.

And so to bed.

Salvatore Quasimodo died of a cerebral hemorrhage.

I shall look as if I were dead, and that will not be true.

Zara Dolukhanova. Irina Arkhipova.

Tchitchikov.

Stein died of cancer of the uterus.

Berthe Morisot was a great-granddaughter of Fragonard.
And married Manet's younger brother.

Judah Halevi was trampled to death by an Arab horseman at the Temple Mount in Jerusalem.
Or died in ways unknown at Damascus.

St. Lawrence was broiled on a gridiron in Rome.
Or was beheaded.

William Ernest Henley died of tuberculosis.

At fifty-nine, George Eliot married a man twenty-one years younger than she.

Who on their Venice honeymoon jumped from a hotel-room balcony into the Grand Canal.

Did Professor Bloom take any books with him, do you know?

Someone said he had a twenty-six-volume complete Joseph Conrad. It's only a weekend cruise.

Conway, New Hampshire, E. E. Cummings died in.

Conway, Massachusetts, Jack Chesbro died in.

Eliot died within months of her wedding, after catching a cold at a concert.

The kingdom of heaven, as described to Rilke by Marina Tsvetayeva after a lifetime of deprivation:

Never again to sweep floors.

Pascal died of abdominal convulsions.

Valéry died of throat cancer.

La Guerre de Troie n'aura pas lieu.

But I always think as we tumble into bed
Of little Willy Wee who is dead, dead, dead.

De Quincey was less than five feet tall.
Hogarth was less than five feet tall.
James Stephens was less than five feet tall.

This is also a kind of verbal fugue, if Writer says so.
If still perhaps less than self-evident to the less than attentive.

B-flat Major, Op. 133.

The realization that Joan was not canonized until two decades into the twentieth century.
Or Thomas More until 1935.

Jesus did not urinate or move his bowels, said Valentinus.

Erasmus died of dysentery.

Luther died of apoplexy.

Mordecai Anielewicz. April 19, 1943:
Nine rifles. Fifty-nine pistols.

These cool blond people make me feel uneasy, said Einstein.
In 1914.

Does Dante want the reader to suspect that Ugolino ate his sons, or not?

I am getting on with my job, said Bernadette of Lourdes.
What is that?
Being ill.

François Boucher died at his easel at sixty-seven.
Painting a backside of Venus.

You can never do too much drawing, Tintoretto said.

In a dramatic, not a narrative form; with incidents
arousing pity and terror.

Nonetheless this is also in many ways even a classic
tragedy, if Writer says so.

> *He is dead and gone, lady,*
>   *He is dead and gone.*

Don't cheer, boys. The poor devils are dying.

As great an artist as ever lived, Mendelssohn called
Jenny Lind.
The greatest singer of us all, Callas called Rosa Ponselle.

William Carlos Williams died after a series of strokes.

John Cheever died of cancer that spread from the kidney to the bone.

Woodlawn Cemetery, in the Bronx, Melville is buried in.

Woodlawn Cemetery, in Toledo, Ohio, Addie Joss is buried in.

Oh, Flask, for one red cherry ere we die!

Is it nothing to you, all ye that pass by?

Disraeli was thoroughly convinced that Mozart was a Jew.

Cagliostro died in a dungeon of the Inquisition.

German beer music, Nietzsche called *Die Meistersinger*.

Sde Boker.

A. E. Housman died of a heart condition.

Shostakovich died of a heart condition.

Café Guerbois.
The Bateau-Lavoir.

News that stays news, Pound identified literature as.

Hectic red.

Henry Adams died of a stroke.

this is not

Addison died of dropsy.

In search of Eldorado.

And of Ophir. Which, still, no one has ever discovered the location of.

Horace's father was a manumitted slave.
Chekhov's grandfather was a serf.

Ivory. Apes. Precious jewels. Peacocks.
Sandalwood.

Bangkok, Thomas Merton died in.
After stumbling into an electric fan while wet from a shower.

Or on the other end of the scale even a volume entitled *Writer's Block*—which Writer is willing to wager some petulant soul will have it.

Depraved May.

Zeno was a pupil of Parmenides.
Who was a pupil of Xenophanes.
Who was a pupil of Anaximander.
Says Diogenes Laërtius.

Kālidāsa was the adopted son of an oxcart driver.

Yossele Rosenblatt.

Jack Dempsey died of a heart attack.

Nelson Algren died of a heart attack.

Congreve died after a coach accident.

Why should we honor those that die upon the field of battle, a man may show as reckless a courage in entering into the abyss of himself.
Said Yeats.

February 23, 1821.
July 8, 1822.
April 19, 1824.

The calamitous last years of Swift:
Labyrinthine vertigo, deafness, paralysis, aphasia, insanity.

Of Carson McCullers:
Stroke, paralysis, heart attack, breast cancer, brain hemorrhage.

Bertrand Russell, at seventy-six, survived an ocean plane crash in which a number of other passengers were killed.

this is not

I know death hath ten thousand several doors
For men to take their exits.
—Says Webster.

James Clarence Mangan. Who died of alcohol or opium
or poverty or neglect.
And is alluded to a dozen times in *Ulysses*.

Giulio Romano.
Who is mentioned in *The Winter's Tale*.

Bizet died of heart disease.

Hobbes died of palsy. At ninety-one.

Russell died at ninety-eight, of bronchial pneumonia.

Janáček died of bronchial pneumonia.

Scott died of the effects of a stroke.

No one ever lacks a good reason for suicide.
Said Cesare Pavese.

The chimney smokes and I leave the room. Why do you
think it a great matter?
Asked Marcus Aurelius.

He was gone in time not to be old.
Said Henry James of Stevenson's death at forty-four.

I have lived long enough: my way of life
Is fall'n into the sear, the yellow leaf.

Smetana died mad. From syphilis.

James died of a stroke.

Gainsborough, on his deathbed, to Joshua Reynolds:
Goodbye till we meet in the hereafter—we and van
Dyck.

Shaw, Kipling, Housman, and Stanley Baldwin were
among Thomas Hardy's pallbearers.

Chaucer may have died of plague.

Sir Philip Sidney died of a sword wound in the thigh.

> *Consider Phlebas, who was once handsome and
> tall as you.*

Lautréamont died of tuberculosis at twenty-four.

Bonington died of tuberculosis at twenty-six.

Delacroix died of what began as a neglected cold.

Wittgenstein played the clarinet.
Lowry played the ukulele.

Emmy Destinn died of a stroke at fifty-one. Toscanini, Puccini, and Caruso had all been in love with her.

Hic jacet Arthurus Rex, quondam Rex que futurus.

The last book Freud read before his death was *La Peau de chagrin* by Balzac.

The last book Kafka read before his death was *Verdi* by Franz Werfel.

A man without feet, walking on his ankles.
Someone insisted having seen at Hiroshima.

There is no drinking after death.
Say Beaumont and Fletcher.

We shall receive no letters in the grave.
Said Johnson.

Samuel Richardson died of a stroke.

Henry Fielding died of dropsy.

There he stood, suffering embarrassment for the mistake of thinking that one may pluck a single leaf from the laurel tree of art without paying for it with his life.

And if thou wilt, remember,
And if thou wilt, forget.

Georges Seurat died of what was probably meningitis.

Does Writer still have headaches? And/or backaches?

As from the start, affording no more than renewed verification that he exists.

In a book without characters.

Not being a character but the author, here.

Turning older or no.

Writer is *writing,* is all. Still.

Chi son? Chi son? Son un poeta.
Che cosa faccio? Scrivo.

The act of painting transforms the painter's mind into something similar to the mind of God.
Said Leonardo.

God, that other craftsman.
Said Picasso.

I am God.
Said Matisse.

—And who are you? said he.—Don't puzzle me; said I.

You are no a de wrider, you are de espider, and we shoota de espiders in Mejico.

Copernicus died of apoplexy.

Rimbaud died of cancer of the bone.
Or of syphilis.

Farewell and be kind.
Say the last words of the original edition of *The Anatomy of Melancholy*.

Farewell as many as wish me well.
Say the last words of *The Unfortunate Traveler*.

El Greco was buried in a Toledo monastery in 1614. Four years later, for reasons not recorded, his body was removed from its vault.
To where, no one has learned since.

Did you ever see anyone die? Well, then I pity you, poor Severn.

Everywhere have I sought peace and found it only in a corner with a book.
Said Thomas à Kempis.

Protagoras died in a shipwreck.

Frater, ave atque vale.

Charleville.

Also there is Writer's tendonitis.

Likewise again merely serving to ratify his existence.

Ben Jonson died partly paralyzed from strokes.
And in penury.

Jane Austen died of what was called neuralgia.
More recent speculation leaning toward lymphoma.

Escritor. Scrittore. Écrivain. Scriptor.

Hugh of Lincoln.
Simon of Trent.

Six centuries after Marathon, Pausanias was still able
to read the names of the Greek dead engraved on columns
at the site.
Eight centuries after the death of Pindar he was able to
visit his tomb in Thebes, still then extant.

And death shall have no dominion.

Grover Cleveland Alexander died alone in a Nebraska
rooming house.

F. Scott Fitzgerald, as seen by John O'Hara in the year
or two before his death:

A prematurely little old man haunting bookshops unrecognized.

Madame, all stories, if continued far enough, end in death.
Said Hemingway.

Longfellow, Emerson, James Russell Lowell, Oliver Wendell Holmes, and Franklin Pierce were among Nathaniel Hawthorne's pallbearers.

Timor mortis conturbat me.
The fear of death distresses me.

Emerson also later attended Longfellow's funeral, but after his own lights had dimmed:
The gentleman we have just been burying was a sweet and beautiful soul; but I forget his name.

Life consists in what a man is thinking of all day.

Watching the burning of Carthage in the Third Punic War, Scipio the Younger quoted Homer on the fall of Troy—and then wept.
At realization of Rome's own mortality, Polybius says.

Longevity all too often means not a long life, but a long death.
Said Democritus.

We ought to leave when the play grows wearisome.
Said Cicero.

Likewise Writer's pinched nerve.

We always find something, eh Didi, to give us the impression we exist?

I *am* real! said Alice, and began to cry.

Cervantes died of diabetes.
Or of cirrhosis of the liver.

Blake died of gallstones.

Scipio the Younger having been a grandson, not a son.

The hearsay, first recorded by a Stratford vicar fifty years later, that Shakespeare died of a fever after a night's carousing with Jonson and Michael Drayton.

Dostoievsky died of a lung hemorrhage.

Tolstoy died of pneumonia, with a nudge from age.

Sir Thomas Browne's will asked that his copy of Horace be placed on his coffin in the grave.

Botticelli spent his last years on crutches.
And on charity.

Botticelli.

Niels Bohr died of a stroke.

Why is there no explanation in Deuteronomy for Moses being made to die after Pisgah and not being permitted to cross over into the Promised Land?

How many People of Israel were there, in the Exodus?

Picasso died of heart failure, in part brought on by acutely congested lungs.

Matisse died after years as an invalid following operations for duodenal cancer.

La Derelitta.

But no man knoweth of his sepulchre unto this day.

Beethoven died of dropsy, after having gone through pneumonia and jaundice.

Franz Grillparzer wrote Beethoven's eulogy. Schubert participated in the funeral.
Twenty months later Grillparzer wrote Schubert's epitaph.

Schwanengesang.

The *Grosse Fuge.*

The lyf so short, the craft so long to lerne.

So many are dead that were young.

Or yet again, Writer's sciatica.

Plato died at eighty or eighty-one, while attending a wedding.

The sun is larger than the Peloponnesus.
Allowed Anaxagoras.

This story of Jesus has helped us a lot.
Allowed Pope Leo X.

Or sometimes of course even a comedy of a sort, if Writer says so.

Death's Jest-Book.

Only three people followed Stendhal's bier.
His longest obituary contained three lines.
One misspelled his name.

Three.

There is no contemporary reference to François Villon after January of 1463, when he was thirty-two and had already at least twice been arrested for having killed.

Nothing has ever modified the assumption that he died either at blade thrust or on a gallows, however.

François Villon.

Some few decades after its opening, the bones of Voltaire and Rousseau were stolen from the Panthéon. And discarded no one knows where.

St. Teresa of Lisieux died of tuberculosis.

St. Teresa of Ávila died of a lung hemorrhage.

Telmetale of stem or stone. Beside the rivering waters of, hitherandthithering waters of.

Or even his synthetic personal *Finnegans Wake,* if Writer so decides.

If only by way of it fitting no other category anyone might suggest.

Timor mortis conturbat me.

It is difficult to find those places today, and you would be no better off if you did, because no one lives there. Said Strabo of the lost past.

Possibly even then thinking of Ophir.

Nobody comes. Nobody calls.

Goethe died of what began as a chest cold.

Emily Dickinson died of Bright's disease.

And how dieth the wise man? As the fool.

Writer's silent heart attack.

The legend that Pythagoras starved himself to death.

The legend that Diogenes committed suicide simply by holding his breath.

Only against Death shall he call for aid in vain.
Says an *Antigone* chorus *re* man's estate.

It seems to us that spring has gone out of the year.
Said Pericles, honoring war dead.

Dante probably died of malaria.

Raphael died of an unsolved fever.
Or more probably from excessive bloodletting by his physicians.

Ille hic est Raphael.

Virgil was known to cough blood, presumably from tuberculosis.

Which is almost certainly what killed him.

Sunt lacrimae rerum et mentem mortalia tangunt.

—Says *Aeneid* I. There are tears for passing things, and things mortal touch the mind.

Requiem. Threnody. Dead march.

Dickens died of a paralytic stroke. At dinner.

Mozart died of renal failure from nephritis. Or of a streptococcal infection. Or of rheumatic fever. Or of a cerebral hemorrhage. Or of mercury poisoning. Or of arsenic poisoning. Or of exhaustion.

Or of possible miscalculated bloodletting, like Raphael.

Like Byron.

What artists do cannot be called work.

Wanhope.

Only one person, his secretary, attended Liebniz's funeral.

One.

Writer's right-lung lobectomy and resected ribs.

The sound of water escaping from mill-dams, willows, old rotten planks, slimy posts, and brickwork, I love such things. These things made me a painter, and I am grateful.
Said Constable.

The little Marcel died of bronchial pneumonia, in addition to his eternal asthma.

Bach died of a stroke.

Donne died of consumption.

When the city I extol shall have perished, when the men to whom I sing shall have faded into oblivion, my words shall remain.
Said Pindar.

Non omnis moriar. I shall not wholly die.
Said Horace.

Per saecula omnia vivam. I shall live forever.
Said Ovid.

Yis-ga-dal v'yis-ka-dash sh'may rab-bo.

Tell me, I pray thee, how fares the human race? If new roofs be risen in the ancient cities? Whose empire is it that now sways the world?

this is not

—Asked one of the fourth-century desert monks, the names of most forever unrecorded.

The time is close when you will have forgotten all things; and when all things will have forgotten you.
Said Marcus Aurelius.

Western wind, when will thou blow
The small rain down can rain?

It is the business of the novelist to create characters.
Said Alphonse Daudet.

Action and plot may play a minor part in a modern novel, but they cannot be entirely dispensed with.
Said Ortega.

If you can do it, it ain't bragging.

Or was it possibly nothing more than a fundamentally recognizable genre all the while, no matter what Writer averred?

Nothing more or less than a *read*?

Simply an unconventional, generally melancholy though sometimes even playful now-ending read?

About an old man's preoccupations.

Dizzy Dean died of a heart attack.

Writer's cancer.

> *Christ, if my love were in my arms*
> *And I in my bed again!*

Then I go out at night to paint the stars.
Says a van Gogh letter.

Farewell and be kind.